ONE BULLET

Casey Wolfe

When Ethan Brant was shot, he found himself dealing with severe PTSD and unable to do his job as a police officer any longer. With the aid of Detective Shawn Greyson, the man who saved his life, Ethan not only finds himself again but discovers love as well.

Shawn's life growing up was less than ideal, however, he overcame that to become who he is today. That doesn't mean he isn't missing something in his life. What Shawn hadn't realized, upon first meeting, was that Ethan could give him all that and more.

One bullet changed both their lives.

Published by
NineStar Press
PO Box 91792
Albuquerque, New Mexico, 87199
www.ninestarpress.com

Warning: This book contains descriptions of a shooting, which is only suitable for mature readers.

Print ISBN # 978-1-945952-82-1
Cover by Natasha Snow
Edited by BJ Toth

DEDICATION

To my mom,
who taught me never to give up,
and my husband,
who never let me.

CHAPTER ONE

Blood. So much blood. The echo of a gun. The smell of gunpowder. The sharp bite of a bullet. Viscous liquid slipping through his fingers.

Darkness. A voice coming through it. Words he should have recognized. Concerned, though not panicked. Surprisingly warm. Warm like the arms he was pulled into.

Flashing lights. Red. Red seen behind closed eyes. Like the blood on his hands, on the ground.

Cold. Like death.

Shooting up in bed, Ethan's anguished cry died on his lips. He shook, breath ragged as he wiped away the cold sweat from his brow. More sweat covered his body, making goosebumps break out. His mouth was dry, throat sore from screaming. No doubt the neighbors would be complaining to building management again.

He wasn't sure how long it took before his brain provided the vital information that he'd been dreaming. Ethan drew in a deep, shaky breath, letting it out slowly. He sat up fully, repeating the process and attempting to calm himself. *It was a dream. Just a dream,* he reminded himself. *You're safe. You're alive. Just a dream.*

When he felt that he wasn't about to go into a full-blown panic attack at any moment, Ethan looked at his bedside clock. The glowing blue numbers informed him there wasn't much point in attempting sleep again. Instead, he switched off the alarm and hauled himself out of bed, trudging toward the bathroom and a cold shower.

He pressed a hand to the tiles, leaning into the spray, head down. As water sloshed off his body, Ethan blew out a breath. He rubbed his free hand over his face before shaking his head as though he could shake out the memories. Sighing, he ran his fingers through his brunet hair. It was looking shabby and in need of a trim, but he couldn't find it in himself to care.

He was losing some muscle as well. Much of that was due to his recovery after being in the hospital. He hadn't been able to run with his parkour buddies until recently or do anything remotely resembling a sit-up. Still, becoming a twenty-six-year-old recluse wasn't doing him any good either.

Ethan wasn't vain, but he did like to stay in shape. His core was still there, even being as out of sorts as he was. Fingers ran across the small scar to the left of his navel, a reminder of the event months before that continued to shadow his every move.

Shutting the shower off, he grabbed a towel and dried his hair the best he could before wrapping the fabric around his waist. Water dripped onto the floor, but he paid it no mind, stopping at the sink to brush his teeth. He caught his reflection in the mirror, his dark-green eyes looking back, haunted.

It was going to be a long day.

* * *

The walk to work wasn't far—roughly half a mile—so Ethan never found a point in taking public transport. Besides, the fresh air did him good. Well, as *fresh* as the air could be in the city. In any case, it was good for him to stretch his legs and clear his head. Unless the weather was poor, he gladly took the extra time to walk, and today was a clear and balmy summer day typical of Washington State.

Perhaps given how his day had started, he should have caught the bus. This was evident the second he looked up and saw a beat cop walking down the sidewalk toward him. Ethan froze momentarily. He tugged at the single strap across his chest, shifting the bag on his back. His eyes darted about, checking traffic and slipping across the street before the cop reached him.

The move must have looked suspicious as Ethan found himself approached by a police cruiser. It paced alongside him, and the officer in the passenger seat called out to him. "Hey, buddy."

Ethan bit back the *I'm not your buddy* that was on the tip of his tongue and, instead, ignored him until the officer raised his voice. "Yeah?" he inquired, not stopping.

"Mind if we chat a minute?"

"Yeah, I do," Ethan answered, turning sideways to slide past some people. "I need to get to work."

"It'll just take a minute," the officer insisted in a tone meant to make him obey.

It was too bad that it didn't work on someone like Ethan. Having been a cop himself, he knew the tricks. He also knew the law. There was no probable cause for them to detain him, so he needn't stop at all. "Sorry. Can't help you."

The cruiser stopped, the officer getting out and moving into his path. "Sir." Ethan backpedaled a few steps. He held up an arm, making a barrier between himself and the cop. He noted the man's partner getting out of the driver's side, walking to the back of the cruiser, and hovering there.

"Officer," Ethan spoke as clearly as he could, "my name is Ethan Brant. There are standing orders within the department that any contact with me should be reported into dispatch immediately." He was attempting to stay calm, but it was difficult as his muscles started to twitch.

The cop stepped forward. "Wait, wait, no..." Ethan began to panic, backing away. He was trying to get out the prepared speech as he was told to say it. Neither of the officers seemed as though they wanted to listen. "You're not supposed to touch me. You're supposed to keep your distance and call it in. Please."

The moment a hand was laid on him, Ethan snapped. He shoved the cop away, taking off at a dead run.

A car slammed its brakes just in time to avoid hitting him, blocking his path. Instinct took over and Ethan slid right across the hood. He could hear the call for backup, but all he wanted was to vanish.

Free running with his friends may have been something he hadn't done much since his accident, thanks to his long recovery, but muscle memory kicked in, and he let his mind go.

He ran between shops, a dumpster on the lowered backlot catching his eye. He cleared the safety railing without slowing, running across the top of the dumpster. With momentum, Ethan leapt off the other side, flipping before landing lightly on his feet.

He came out of the connecting alley into a shopping plaza, wide open for him to work with. Ethan made to turn left, spotting the cruiser that screamed up onto the sidewalk. In midrun he extended his foot out, springing off a bench and pushing his body in the opposite direction. Using the retaining wall of the decorative plant beds to avoid the crowd, he managed to get distance between them.

Ahead there was a set of stairs going down toward the park, and rather than avoid them, he used the terrain to his advantage. Diving forward, he cleared the stone rail, his palms touching the rail on the opposite side. He tucked his legs, missing both rails as he swung them forward, feet landing lightly on the ground. Despite protesting muscles, he repeated the same move for the next stairway.

As he kept running, he realized where he was. It didn't matter that another set of cops had come in from the opposite end of the shopping plaza because Ethan wasn't planning to use the traditional entrance. A brick wall with a switchback of stairs was at his right, and that was his means of escape.

Forgetting the stairs—which would only slow him down—he brought his left foot up to a railing, using it to launch him at the wall. He gripped the ledge above him, bringing his knees up to push with the balls of his feet. Muscling up made him grunt at the pain coursing through his abdomen, a move he shouldn't have been doing just yet.

Somewhere in the back of his head, he was aware of the cops yelling in disbelief, getting their colleagues on the radio to update them on Ethan's direction of travel. Ethan didn't plan on the police being able to find him fast enough before he completely disappeared.

He ran across the street, jumping up and over the wooden bench in his path. Well aware of the laptop in his backpack, rather than simply tucking and rolling, he shifted his weight midair so he would land on his hip and leg, rolling through to his feet.

The entrance to the subway was right there, and he slid down the metal railing in the center of the stairwell.

Ethan's breathing was ragged. It had been too long since he had a run like that; his muscles burned. He leaned a forearm on a pillar, waiting for the next train to pass through the subway. He just needed to sit, to center himself. A crowded morning train car wasn't the best place, but he didn't have much of a choice.

Even the strap of his backpack felt constraining across his chest. He yanked the strap over his head and set the bag onto the ground at his feet. Ethan took a deep lungful of air.

Just as he thought he was safe, someone grabbed his arm. Ethan simply reacted, using his strength to swing the man around to collide with the pillar. It was then Ethan saw his attacker was a cop, but he missed the officer's partner.

Volts of electricity cascaded through his body, causing Ethan's legs to buckle, and he went down on the tiled platform. He was helpless to stop the officer who put a knee in his back, grabbing his arms. Panic seeped into every pore. The click of the handcuffs as the cold metal wrapped around his wrist made him struggle. It was in vain; a second shocking jolt was sent through him.

"Get off him!" a man ordered. "Now!" It took Ethan a moment to recognize the smooth cadence and authoritative tone. He craned his neck, tears stinging his eyes, to gaze on Detective Shawn Greyson. When the officers protested, Shawn held up his badge and glowered. "Stand down," he growled, physically removing them.

"We just chased this kid all over the damn city!" one argued. "Just 'cause yer a detective—"

"I said back off!" Shawn yelled, eyes like fire and his entire presence radiating danger. It was more than enough to have both of them doing as they were told.

Shawn immediately crouched next to Ethan and unhooked the cuffs. Shawn helped him to sit, running his hands up and down Ethan's arms. "Hey, you're alright. You're safe," Shawn assured him, voice low and easy. Ethan met deep blue-gray eyes, heart-wrenching at the sight of the friendly face. "Just focus on your breathing, okay? I've got you."

Ethan nodded, thankful for the watchful gaze that allowed him to concentrate on centering himself. He listened to Shawn's steady voice, not even focusing on the words so much as the calming tone. Shawn's touch was reassuring, hands continuing their path up and down Ethan's arms before grasping his shoulders.

"That's it," Shawn spoke. "There you go." Ethan took a deep breath, looking at him once more. Shawn smiled encouragingly. "Better?" Ethan gave a slight nod, not trusting his voice just yet. "Okay. Take your time."

Shawn shifted a little closer, a comforting presence where normally being near people would make things worse. Ethan never questioned why that was, and he wasn't about to start. He allowed Shawn to help him to his feet, the extra couple inches the detective had on him making Ethan look up to meet his eyes.

Despite Shawn's superior height, Ethan had the broader frame. Not that Shawn was a slouch—far from it. He could have sat on his laurels as a detective, but rather than let himself go, the thirty-two-year-old only worked that much harder in everything he did. It was one of the many things Ethan had come to admire about the man.

"Thank you," Ethan murmured, finding his voice.

"Don't mention it," Shawn replied, lips pulling into that little smirk of his. On others, it would be infuriating. On Shawn, it was endearing.

Realizing he was staring, Ethan quickly looked away. "I did everything you told me!" he blurted, wanting to explain himself. He knew Shawn would listen, would understand. It was amazing what Shawn picked up on without any need for words.

Shawn shushed him gently. "It's okay," he assured Ethan. "Let's get you down to the station to give your statement and—"

"No way in hell," Ethan refused, shaking his head as he tried to back away.

Before he could bolt, Shawn snagged his arm. "Relax, relax." Shawn sighed, running his free hand through short strawberry-blond curls. He clearly noticed Ethan was still tense as he appeased him by saying, "Forget it. Lemme take you home."

"Really?" Ethan finally relaxed. The idea of going to a police station, especially after what just happened, wasn't appealing in the least. The fact he didn't even have to explain any of this to Shawn was greatly appreciated. "Yeah. Yeah, okay," he agreed.

Ethan grabbed his discarded backpack. His arms still felt a bit like gelatin from the Taser hit. Really, he was just thankful the officer had been using a handheld version without probes. Digging those out was a pain, and Ethan had no desire to deal with medics either.

Shawn ushered him outside to a black Chrysler 300 that was haphazardly parked in the fire lane, built-in red and blue light strips flashing. The door was even wide open, telling Ethan just how quickly Shawn had jumped to his rescue. The admiration he held for Shawn continued to grow, barely trumping the feelings of guilt at being such a bother.

"Come on. Get in," Shawn urged. He pressed his palm to Ethan's lower back, directing him toward the passenger side while ignoring the small crowd that had gathered to curiously gawk.

Ethan opened the door, hesitating when he saw Shawn lock onto the officers who had followed them out. "I expect copies of all the incident reports sent to Captain Sanchez by the end of the day. For everyone who was involved." Shawn's expression held no room for argument, his sharp jawline and narrowed eyes creating quite the menacing appearance when he wanted it to.

Shawn slipped into the car then, waiting until Ethan followed suit before backing out, switching off the lights when they were underway. "You're still up on Oakes, right?" Shawn inquired.

"Yeah," he answered, fidgeting a bit. The leather seats were nice—the whole car was, actually. He hadn't even realized he'd spoken out loud until Shawn grinned over at him. "Thanks for the save," Ethan repeated.

"Told ya not to mention it." The smile still on Shawn's face softened the scolding. After making a turn, Shawn inquired, "So what happened?"

"I did everything like you said," Ethan mumbled. "Didn't seem to matter."

Shawn nodded slowly.

They had discussed a plan last time they had seen each other, after a similar run-in with uniformed officers that had Ethan ready to freak out. Shawn offered up what he felt would be a solution—identifying himself, asking that they not touch him, and telling them to radio dispatch for further instructions.

"I wrote the memo that went out to the department myself," Shawn groused, pursing his lips together in obvious displeasure. "It was made rather clear there was a former officer with PTSD who was supposed to be approached with caution." He huffed, "Apparently not clear enough." By the tone, Ethan could tell *that* was going to be corrected rather colorfully.

When they parked in front of his building, Ethan unbuckled and gazed over at Shawn. "If I say 'thank you' again, are you gonna smack me?"

Shawn's grin said it all. Instead of answering, Shawn jerked his chin for Ethan to get out before shutting off the car and reaching for the door. Confused, Ethan grabbed his bag from the floorboard and jumped out. "Let's get you inside and settled" was all Shawn said as he walked around to meet him on the sidewalk.

"You don't have to—"

"Humor me," Shawn insisted, cutting Ethan off as he steered him toward the building entrance.

Ethan relented, allowing Shawn to escort him upstairs. Even so, as he let Shawn into his simple apartment, Ethan mentioned, "You didn't really have to do this. I'll be fine."

"I know you will be. Just better to have someone around while you come back down." Shawn shrugged it off casually, but Ethan couldn't help but wonder how he seemed to know so much about PTSD. Then again, the man had been in the department for a long time, so it no doubt came with the territory.

Nodding, Ethan walked farther inside, dropping his bag onto the coffee table. "Fuck, I need to call my boss." He was already late, and as it was, he doubted he could pull it together enough to step out his front door for the rest of the day.

"I can call him if you want," Shawn offered. Once again it was as though Shawn could read Ethan's thoughts. Even the idea of talking to another person at the moment was enough to stress him out. For some reason, that didn't seem to extend to Shawn.

"Yeah, alright." He handed Shawn his cell after punching in his boss's direct number.

Apparently Frank was worried about him as the phone picked up right away. "Hello, this is Detective Shawn Greyson. I'm calling in regards to Ethan Brant... No, sir, he's alright. There was an incident with some of our officers, and he's a bit shaken up. I've advised him to stay home for the day." Shawn glanced over at him as Frank talked, Ethan's eyes dancing away out of embarrassment. "Of course, sir, I'll let him know. Thank you for being so understanding."

Shawn offered the phone back, their fingers brushing as Ethan took it. "He says to take the time you need and to give him a call when you feel up to it." He paused before commenting, "A very reasonable guy." Ethan had made Shawn aware that his new boss was in the know about his PTSD. Given Shawn's reaction, he sounded impressed with the delicate way Frank handled the matter.

Ethan flinched as Shawn stepped closer to him. It was just a sensory reaction and no reflection on Shawn. Even so, Shawn frowned and seemed to debate backing away. "Sorry," Ethan murmured, giving Shawn the courage to take another step forward instead.

"It's okay. Really." Shawn reached out slowly, being careful with his movements, and taking hold of his chin. "Lemme see that." He tilted Ethan's face so he could view the damage to his right cheekbone that Ethan could only feel. "Well, it's gonna bruise but no broken skin." Ethan nodded, dislodging Shawn's hand in the process. "Did you take your meds today?"

That earned a glare from Ethan as he backed away and flopped onto the couch. "I don't wanna be on that shit anymore. Makes me feel out of it... Been doin' okay without them. Just, some days, shit happens."

Letting out a soft sigh Ethan didn't think he was supposed to hear, Shawn took a seat on the couch next to him. Shawn was careful to keep some space between them. "Did something else happen?" he inquired, tilting his head slightly. There was nothing accusatory there; rather, Ethan felt comforted by the concern.

It caused Ethan to confess, "Had nightmares last night." He pulled a leg up to his chest, resting his arm on it. "About that night."

Shawn frowned, nodding in understanding. It naturally explained a lot. Reliving the shooting always caused Ethan to be skittish, a sure way to draw attention. Contact with cops was the last thing Ethan had needed today: the perfect storm of events.

Shawn asked, out of the blue, "How can you be so relaxed around me?" Ethan gave him a curious look. "I'm a *cop*," Shawn pointed out the obvious. "Shouldn't that freak you out? Especially now?"

Ethan blinked at that, looking off into thin air. It was a fair point. "But," he answered softly, "you're the one that saved me." As far as Ethan was concerned, that was everything.

He supposed the fact Shawn was a detective rather than a uniformed officer had a little to do with it as well. After all, it wasn't so in-your-face. His badge was slipped into an inner pocket. His gun was tucked away in a shoulder holster, usually hidden by the trench coat he wore for work. True, his appearance screamed of power, but Shawn dressed with class rather than anything that labeled him *law enforcement*.

Silence settled between them, obviously Shawn thinking about what Ethan had said. Ethan cleared his throat, unfolding himself. "I should probably get some work done."

In truth, Ethan could get a majority of his workload done from home since most of it was computer-based anyway. His new position as a consultant for a high-tech security firm allowed him the flexibility to work from just about anywhere. Even so, Ethan was well aware locking himself away wouldn't do his mental health any favors.

"I'll get out of your hair," Shawn offered as he stood. "Call me if you need anything."

Ethan assured him he would, though there was no missing the skeptical look on Shawn's face before he left.

* * *

Taking one look at his desk, Shawn heaved a sigh. He only gave the sticky notes stuck to his computer monitor a cursory glance before dropping his leather satchel on the floor. He shrugged out of his trench coat, throwing it across the short filing cabinet next to his desk before flopping down into his rolling chair. Just thinking of all the paperwork he had to do after closing that case the previous day was making his head hurt. He may have had it done already if he hadn't been waylaid.

Shawn mentally scolded himself. It wasn't Ethan's fault, and the man certainly had needed him. That was all that mattered. When he'd heard Ethan's name go out over the radio as a runner, he hadn't even given it a second thought before joining the chase. There was something about the guy; Shawn felt obligated to him in a way, felt a deep need to protect him.

So he had to work a couple extra hours—nothing new. He didn't have any pressing cases at the moment anyway. With that settled, he simply rolled up his sleeves and got to work.

Not that he was left in peace for long. Detective Richard Davies strolled over, leaning a hip against one side of Shawn's L-shaped desk. "Do you ever even *look* at your desk?" Davies griped. It was good-natured enough, but Shawn wasn't in the mood and thus only grunted. "Seriously, how do you find anything?"

Shawn lowered his brows, looking up at the towering blond in annoyance. "Did you need something Dick, or did you just come over here to bitch about my cleaning?"

"Well someone's in a pissy mood," he huffed, taking a drink of his coffee before inquiring, "What's got your panties in a bunch?"

Snorting, Shawn turned back to his case file and the related report. "Don't you have better things to be doing? Like getting a lead on the double homicide from Tuesday night?" He scratched out a few more informational points before looking at Davies, one brow cocked in challenge.

"Did we run outta your tea again, Princess? I mean I know you act like coffee will kill ya, but maybe you should think about trying it." He toasted Shawn with his mug pointedly.

Groaning in obvious frustration, Shawn thunked his head onto the desk. "What do you want?" he demanded again, voice muffled by the papers.

"Maybe I wanted to talk?" He heard Davies plop into one of the cheap seats beside his desk. "Honestly now, what's up with you?" Shawn understood the question, of course. Typically, he would go toe to toe in verbal boxing matches like a pro. Today wasn't one of those days.

Threading his fingers into his strawberry-blond locks, Shawn curled them to tug a bit. Elbows on the desk, he looked up to pin Davies with an expression that could kill. "Not. Now."

"Uh-huh." Davies stopped speaking, and even though he didn't make to leave, Shawn went back to work. However, he didn't miss Davies reaching out to pick up one of the books Shawn had stacked on his desk. "*Living with PTSD*," Davies read. "*Moving on After Trauma, Coping Methods...*" He made a sweeping gesture to the various self-help books and case studies. "This about that kid?"

Heaving a sigh of defeat, Shawn dropped his pen and leaned back in his chair to look across the desk. "I've been doing some homework since Brant was diagnosed, yes." He had in fact been researching various treatment methods and coping techniques in hopes of finding something that could help Ethan.

"For real?" Davies looked skeptical, turning the book over in his hand as though it would reveal some sort of secret. He ended up huffing, tossing it haphazardly onto the desk. "Ain't like he's your problem." Shawn narrowed his eyes. "Can't fix everything that's broken."

"PTSD is nothing to make light of!" Shawn snapped, not appreciating Davies's dismissal.

"I know that," Davies replied, not bothering to check his attitude. "I just don't get what the fuck the kid's problem is. We've all been through shit too. And freaking out every time he sees one of us—"

"It was a *cop* who shot him!" Shawn reminded him, practically seething.

"Greyson—"

"Just fuck off, okay?"

Davies stared at him a long moment before shaking his head. He got up, with a sigh, but to his credit didn't say another word and went back to his own desk. Shawn watched him, eyes hard. It took him a minute to realize how tense he had become and forced himself to take a deep breath to try to forget it.

That was the hard part though—forgetting. Even though it had been Ethan hurt that day, it had been an event that affected Shawn deeply as well.

When he arrived on the scene of a robbery in progress, two uniformed officers were taking off on foot after the suspect. Shawn joined the chase, not far behind.

"I said stop!" one of them yelled.

"Seems like that's really working, Jay," the other cop managed to scoff.

As the suspect turned the corner ahead of them, Jay pointed in that direction. "Hit the alley, Steve, and try to cut him off!"

"Got it." While Steve took a left down the narrow side street, Jay and Shawn kept after the guy, but they were all starting to lose steam.

Coming around the corner, they found the suspect had knocked into someone, tripping him up. It allowed them to gain some ground. However, when the man went to turn down another street, Jay wasn't about to let him get away and drew his gun.

That's when the unthinkable happened.

The robber ran into another man who was walking down the sidewalk, from around the corner where no one could see. It was the same moment that Jay fired, Shawn having yelled too late for him to stop. The hit from the robber sent the innocent bystander straight into the path of the bullet.

"Fuck!" Jay cursed, Shawn not stopping as he went to the aid of the young man now kneeling on the sidewalk in shock.

Steve had managed to come out ahead of the suspect, tackling him to the pavement. Jay slowed next to Shawn, eyes widened. "Help him," Shawn ordered, jerking his chin toward the pair wrestling on the ground.

Shawn got down on one knee, radioing dispatch that they needed an ambulance. The brunet in front of him looked at Shawn in a daze, hand on his abdomen where he'd been shot. "I think... I think I'm gonna be sick," he mentioned before swaying and losing his balance.

"Hang on, kid," Shawn urged, catching him before he hit the ground. The man coughed, groaning in pain. Shawn didn't know what else to do other than attempt to slow the bleeding. That was how Shawn ended up with the victim cradled in his lap, a hand pressed tightly to his stomach.

"Hey," Shawn encouraged him, "Hey, look at me." A terrified gaze met his. "You're gonna be okay. What's your name?"

"Ethan," he managed.

Shawn noticed him trying to grab something in his pocket and fished it out for him. What he found made his heart stop. In his hand was a badge. The guy was a fellow officer. "Step up that bus!" Shawn ordered into the radio. "We have an officer down."

He looked down at Ethan, attempting to keep him awake. "Ethan, talk to me." When Ethan shook his head, Shawn didn't back down. "Try."

"Thought you were only supposed to get shot on duty," he managed dryly, coughing some more.

The blood squished through Shawn's fingers, and he cursed internally. Where was that ambulance? He wasn't going to let this kid die on him. Shawn only held firmer, not missing the wince that crossed Ethan's face. "I'm sorry. I have to try an' stop the bleeding."

"I feel cold."

That made Shawn go cold next. "Just the adrenaline," he lied, free hand carding through Ethan's hair in comfort. "Your body doesn't want you to feel pain."

"Still hurts," Ethan grunted in return.

"I know."

Ethan's hand came up, falling on top of Shawn's, more blood oozing out. "Don't leave me," he pleaded, consciousness drifting.

"I won't," Shawn promised without any thought.

He heard the sirens, having missed their approach earlier while he was distracted by keeping Ethan calm and awake. When the medics jumped out, there was a flurry of activity, but not once did Shawn leave the young man's side.

Shawn could still remember the ambulance ride to the hospital, how pale Ethan had become. He'd barely been hanging onto consciousness, and watching him fight through the fog hadn't been easy. Perhaps that was why Shawn had held onto Ethan's hand as he attempted to keep out of the medic's way.

Despite being covered in blood, Shawn hadn't gone home. Something had compelled him to stay, to be sure Ethan made it through.

It had taken a few hours, but when the surgeon had come out to meet Shawn, she had good news. The bullet had caused quite a bit of damage—mainly ripping apart Ethan's intestines, sending bacteria swimming around in his body—however, they'd been able to locate and repair what they needed. Ethan's heart had stopped at one point, and they'd shocked him multiple times with a defibrillator to bring him back. Overall, though, Ethan's chances had seemed good.

He had been surprised at the offer to see Ethan, but Shawn hadn't turned it down.

Shawn was brought to a private room in the SICU, machines beeping softly and various bags of fluids hanging on an IV pole. He pulled a chair up to the bedside, sitting slowly as he gazed at Ethan, who was still feeling the effects of the anesthesia. After the nurse left them, Shawn offered a forced smile. "Hey," he greeted, "looks like you made it."

"Yeah." Ethan's voice was a little rough but he smiled back. "They said you saved my life."

"Just doing my job," he answered, hand falling on Ethan's forearm. "It's everybody else you should thank."

It was a half-truth. The surgeon had informed him that without Shawn's immediate intervention, Ethan might not have made it. Still, Shawn didn't see it as being praiseworthy to simply do the right thing; it was something anyone else would have done.

"You don't take praise real well, huh?" Ethan sounded teasing, and Shawn couldn't help but chuckle and shake his head. "Seriously though, just take the thanks, okay?"

"Okay," Shawn agreed, squeezing Ethan's arm.

When the nurse returned with a variety of medications to inject into the IV, Shawn took the time to really look at Ethan. He had color in his face again, which was good, and his dark-green eyes were looking brighter as the anesthesia was wearing off. His hair was crusted with blood—apparently the staff had forgotten about it while cleaning Ethan up—and Shawn was reminded he was the one to put it there.

"Well, I should probably go," Shawn mentioned once the nurse was finished. "Let you get some sleep."

"Yeah..." Ethan murmured, already a little drowsy from the meds. "Yeah, okay. Thanks."

Shawn patted Ethan's arm when he stood, although he hesitated as he looked down at the broken young man. "They called somebody for you, right? Your family?"

Ethan gave a halfhearted shrug. "Doubt they got anyone."

Frowning, Shawn offered, "Well, I'll see you tomorrow then." Ethan seemed understandably confused. Shawn couldn't stand the thought of someone being all alone in a hospital, especially under such dire circumstances.

"You don't have to do that," Ethan replied, giving him a way out.

Shawn gave him a little smile. "No trouble," he assured him before starting to walk out.

Ethan's voice stopped him in the doorway. "Hey. What's yer name?"

He looked back, smile growing. "Shawn. Shawn Greyson."

There was a sleepy smile in reply. "Thanks, Shawn."

The memory of that fateful night was a mix of emotion, even after so much time. A strange bond had formed between them. It just seemed natural for Shawn to keep up with Ethan's progress as he was recovering. And when Ethan had been diagnosed with PTSD—something that didn't surprise Shawn in the least—it was Shawn who'd tried to help him.

Benched by the department until he was psychologically cleared, Ethan, instead, had turned in his badge. Shawn wasn't about to begrudge him that. He was the last person who wanted anyone poking around in his head.

With a frustrated huff, Shawn snagged his satchel and dropped it with a *thunk* onto his desk. He needed to get his mind on work. There were forensic results sitting in his inbox that he needed to go over, and he had to check with the captain to see if there was a new assignment waiting for him. Although Captain Sanchez was liable to kick him out of his office since—as he said constantly—he would come to Shawn with any work that needed to be done, *"So get the hell out."*

Perhaps he did work too much as his colleagues claimed. However, no one could ever accuse him of not doing his job.

Having moved north from the Seattle area, Shawn was still not all that far from where he'd grown up—less than an hour's drive. Smaller than Seattle, Cape Cascara was still sizeable enough to warrant a police force of a couple hundred, not even including their near dozen detectives. Their headquarters was the largest, but the two satellite stations were nothing to sneeze at; it had been one of those where Ethan had been stationed, while Shawn worked with the other detectives at Main.

Part of the reason behind their size was their location on the Puget Sound. It was alive with the commercial fishing industry and people working blue-collar jobs at various manufacturing plants. It even found its share of tourism thanks to the Sound and the islands in it. With mountains and national forest on the other side, Cape Cascara was an interesting place to live.

Shawn loved his city. And he would do anything to see it be a safe and happy place to live. Perhaps it was a naïve ambition. Yet that didn't stop him from putting his head down and getting to work.

CHAPTER TWO

Ethan paused the DVR when there was a knock at the door. He wasn't quite expecting Shawn to be on the other side. "Hey," Ethan greeted, moving aside to let him pass. "Whaddaya doin' here?"

"I feel the love," Shawn remarked, smirking as he set a paper bag on the kitchen counter right inside the door.

Ethan managed a smile, shaking his head before moving over to peer inside the bag. "What's this?"

"Figured you might not feel up to cooking tonight, so..." He pulled out a small rotisserie chicken. "Thought I'd bring you some dinner."

"You didn't have to do this," Ethan replied, watching as a container of mac-n-cheese, followed by green beans, was put on the counter.

Shawn shrugged. "I know, but you still have to eat. Not like it was out of my way."

Ethan knew that to be an outright lie. Even so, he gave Shawn a grateful smile. "Well if ya haven't eaten yet," he offered, "care to join me?"

Shawn agreed, "I could eat."

Ethan moved around Shawn and into the tiny kitchen. The wraparound countertop was the only thing separating it from the remaining living area of the apartment. The living room and small dining room merged together, stressing a need for organization in such an economic space.

It was only a one-bedroom apartment. While it was more than enough room for him, after coming home from the hospital, it had been a little crowded with his family there. The pullout couch had served as a bed for his parents, while his little brother, Matt, had shared his queen bed—the one luxury in his home besides the large, flat-screen TV.

Ethan grabbed a couple of plates and silverware, tilting his head toward the small square table. It may have had four chairs, but whoever thought it was big enough for that many people to dine at was sadly mistaken. It wouldn't be bad with just the two of them though.

"So, how was yer day?" Ethan inquired casually, as he set the table, Shawn following with the food. "Hope I didn't get you in trouble."

"Not at all," Shawn assured him, offering a brief, lopsided smile. "And it was...well..." He shrugged, taking off his trench coat and putting it over the back of his chair. There was no missing the fact that Shawn's shoulder holster was absent, and Ethan could only guess his firearm had been left in the car.

"That exciting, huh?" Ethan teased, going to grab some bottles of water from the fridge; he really had to go shopping.

Shawn barked out a laugh, taking a seat. "Oh yes. Another day of sifting through forensic evidence and going over witness statements to try to piece together the latest crime we've got to solve."

Ethan took the seat across from him, and they both started dishing out food. "But you like yer job, yeah?"

They'd never really talked about Shawn's profession, given the delicate subject of law enforcement, in general, with Ethan. After getting to know Shawn, however, it seemed like a safe enough topic to get into. Besides, Ethan would have to learn how to deal with it if he was going to continue the friendship they had been tentatively building since the shooting.

"I love it," Shawn confirmed, his features softening as he settled in. "I get to help people. As cheesy as it sounds." His smile made him look almost boyish as he talked, a clear glow about him. "Most people, I meet them on the worst days of their lives. I want to help them." He gave a little shrug in an attempt to downplay it. "If by catching the *bad guy,* I can bring them some peace, well..."

Ethan couldn't help but smile, looking down at his plate as he replied, "Well, you sure helped me." He stabbed at some mac-n-cheese, glancing up to find Shawn looking at him thoughtfully.

In the end, Shawn didn't respond; rather, he started to eat. After a few moments of silence, though, he flipped the question back. "Did you get everything done today?"

"Didn't really have much to do. Had to sign off on some things and talk to a customer about bundling in some new services." Ethan shrugged. "May have to go out on a new contract next week."

Most of Ethan's job involved making sure plans were in place that fit their clients' needs. Between his business degree and law-enforcement background, his boss had seen what an asset he could be. Ethan had a natural talent with people and an eye for details that made him the perfect fit to go out and meet new clients: typically, of the large, corporate variety.

"Out of town?"

"Yeah, but won't have to stay overnight. Frank's good about avoiding that. Don't really know about being away from home like that right now."

"I'm sure you'd be fine." Apparently noticing the little tick of Ethan's face, Shawn quickly changed topics. "How's the family?" It was an interesting choice since Ethan knew full well Shawn was estranged with most of his own family, unlike the close relationship Ethan shared with his.

"Mom's still bugging me to come home. And Matty's totally on her side."

"You don't want to?"

"Not just yet. I need to get resettled, y'know? Besides, if I go home...I dunno that I'd come back."

"Well we can't have that," Shawn teased, a smile playing on his lips. "I'm getting used to having you around."

Ethan chuckled, shaking his head. "Not sure I've really made the best impression, so I guess that's saying something."

"*Please*, I'm a pain in the ass, so you're pretty perfect in my book." Ethan looked away quickly, feeling a blush form as he ducked his head. Apparently missing it, Shawn asked, "So you have any plans this weekend?"

"Was thinking of meeting up with some friends during the day. Otherwise nothing. Why?"

Shawn shrugged casually, sipping his water. "This was nice, having food together. Thought maybe we could do it again. Hang out. I can cook for you."

Ethan smirked. "Not about to turn down a free meal."

"That's settled then. Saturday evening alright?"

"Sounds like a plan."

The rest of the meal was spent with easy banter, Ethan finding he could be himself without worry. It was a novelty to Shawn—or so he said—and Ethan really needed the extra comfort of a friendly face these days.

Having cleared the table, Ethan was running water in the sink when he looked over at Shawn. "So, umm, I've been meaning to ask..."

When he didn't continue, Shawn prompted, "Shoot." There was no missing the immediate cringe that followed.

That actually made Ethan laugh. He appreciated the thought, but he wasn't made of spun glass. "No need to tiptoe 'round me there, Greyson."

"Believe you were asking something," Shawn reminded him.

"Nice save."

Shawn inclined his head, managing a half smile in return.

"So, like I was sayin', been supposed to ask ya... My therapist has been buggin' me. She wants to see if you'll sit in on a session."

"Me?"

Ethan nodded, unsure why he felt nervous all of a sudden.

"Well, yeah, sure," Shawn continued. "But why would she want *me* there?"

Ethan picked up the wash rag to start on dishes so he wouldn't have to look at Shawn while he admitted, "Well she knows about you, obviously. Guess she thinks that she might get some insight from you or something."

"Mm-hmm..." Shawn didn't sound particularly convinced. All the same, he said, "Yeah, I'm game. Just lemme know when." There was a pause before Shawn nudged Ethan's hip. "Here, gimme that." He held out his hand for the rag. "I'll wash. You dry and put away."

"Nope. You took care of dinner. I'll take care of dishes."

Shawn nudged him more insistently that time. "Ain't like I cooked it, so scoot over."

Ethan gave in that time, begrudgingly, and moved aside, grabbing the dish towel. "Pushy bastard."

"Damn straight." Shawn didn't bother hiding his smile.

That made Ethan grin as well, just happy to see Shawn happy. It wasn't a completely foreign concept to Ethan—wanting to be the reason someone else was happy—though it had been a while since that had been the case. Watching Shawn scrub dishes in his kitchen, Ethan could feel the stirring of something inside him, which both exhilarated and terrified him.

* * *

The door to the office opened, and a middle-aged brunette stepped partially out to look in the waiting room. "Ethan," she greeted with a soft smile. "Come on in."

Ethan shoved his hands into his jeans pockets, a bit nervous, given the man who trailed after him that particular day. Shawn, on the other hand, appeared perfectly at ease.

"You must be Detective Greyson," she continued, following them into the office. "Lynn Bowers. But please, call me Lynn."

Shawn gave her an easy smile. "Shawn," he insisted as they shook hands. He took a seat next to Ethan on the comfortable couch, glancing over at him. "You okay?" Shawn inquired, apparently catching his unease. Ethan only nodded, causing a frown to cross Shawn's face.

"Well," Lynn began, sitting in a plush chair near them, rather than behind her desk, "I'm very glad you were able to come. I had asked Ethan if he would like to include you."

"It's no trouble," Shawn answered, glancing over at Ethan once more.

"Have you two discussed the reason for joining us in a session?"

"Not so much," Ethan admitted, leaning into the corner of the couch to get comfortable. He tucked his right foot under his left thigh, allowing him to angle toward them to engage.

Lynn explained to Shawn, "My understanding is that you've been an essential part in his recovery. Would you agree, Ethan?"

Ethan bit his lip. He didn't want Shawn to feel obligated, which was, of course, the biggest reason he'd been avoiding asking him in the first place.

As usual, Lynn caught his mood and asked, "Is it still alright with you if Shawn's involved?"

Ethan picked at a fray in his jeans. "Bit selfish to ask more from him, don't you think?"

"Hey," Shawn protested gently, laying a hand on his knee. "I wouldn't be here if I didn't want to be."

Ethan looked from the hand squeezing his knee up to Shawn's color-changing eyes. In the light of the office, they looked to be a calm gray, and the gentle way Shawn was looking at him set Ethan at ease, just as it always seemed to do.

"Yeah," Ethan finally answered with a nod, feeling a bit more certain about the situation. "Yeah, okay."

"Good?"

"Good," Ethan assured him, quirking his lips in the hint of a smile.

With that settled, Lynn prompted, "So, Ethan, how have you been since our last session?"

"Alright, I guess."

She raised a brow to that. "Just alright?"

"Last week," Ethan confessed, thinking of the subway platform, "I had a panic attack."

Lynn gave a sympathetic hum. "Can you tell me more about what happened?"

"Had a dream."

"What was it about?" she prodded gently when he didn't offer more.

"The shooting."

After another long pause, it was Shawn who supplied, "He ended up having a run-in with a few patrol officers. I took him home afterward."

Lynn offered him a kind smile. "That was nice of you." She crossed her legs, smoothing out her skirt. Glancing between them, Lynn inquired of Ethan, "Have you talked to Shawn about the progress you've made?"

"A little." He looked over at Shawn. "I don't think we've ever gone into detail."

Shawn shook his head. "I figured you'd tell me if it was important for me to know."

Ethan's lips ticked up momentarily.

"Would you like to update him then?" Lynn suggested.

Ethan should have seen that one coming. Having *him* say it made it real. Lynn had pulled the same tactic when Ethan and his mother had come to her the first time. Aileen had nearly broken down in tears. She had highly approved of Lynn—as had Ethan—and so he'd put up little fight when regular sessions were scheduled.

"We've done a lot of work with different relaxation stuff," Ethan said. Shawn sat patiently while Ethan explained the various techniques he was using, both to promote a healthy balance and to calm himself if he started spiraling.

"So what about exposure therapy?" Shawn asked. Designed to help people overcome their past trauma by facing the object of their fears, that meant, for Ethan, being around police officers again.

Ethan managed not to cringe at the very phrase, which he supposed meant it was going well enough. "We've done some in the office."

Shawn's brows lowered in confusion, and Ethan clarified, "Virtual reality. Small doses."

"It's a controlled environment," Lynn added.

"But at some point, he has to get out and do the real thing," Shawn argued. "I think what happened the other day only proves that." Ethan twitched at the reminder.

Lynn inclined her head in agreement. All the same, she replied, "It's a process. Each person has their own pace."

"I know that, but…" Shawn frowned, apparently rethinking what he wanted to say. "Isn't that the point, though? Pushing the comfort zone?"

"Yes, with the goal being to eliminate fear or at the least function with some sense of normality. However, pushing *too* much can ruin what progress we *have* made." Lynn turned her attention back to Ethan. "What are your feelings about moving forward with exposure therapy?"

"Don't need another breakdown," Ethan answered dryly.

Shawn looked over at him, brows lowered. "But you don't know that. You're strong, Ethan. You can do it. I know you can."

Ethan flushed, ducking his head and looking away. "I think you have more confidence than I do" was all he said.

"Well, what about music therapy?" Shawn tried, looking back to Lynn. "That could help, right?"

"It's not a treatment form I've dealt with before," Lynn admitted. "I honestly don't know much about it. Statistically speaking."

"I've done a lot of reading on it. I could send along the case study I have, if you'd like."

She smiled, thanking him for the offer.

Ethan was busy staring at Shawn. He had no idea that Shawn knew any of this sort of thing. That amazement turned to embarrassment, when Shawn continued, "I figure it might be something that would work since Ethan loves music so much."

Shawn's attention returned to him. He was smiling softly at Ethan, warmth radiating from his presence. Ethan couldn't believe everything Shawn had done for him, as it was, but learning that he'd been looking into treatments and worrying about how things were progressing was almost too much. Shawn didn't owe him anything.

Ethan ended up standing, awkwardly excusing himself to go to the restroom.

* * *

Shawn watched Ethan leave, his focus pulled to Lynn when she commented, "You know, you're a frequent topic in our sessions."

"I am?" He didn't bother to hide his surprise.

"You're a solid presence in his life right now. Ethan doesn't really have anyone else to turn to."

Confused, Shawn replied, "I know he doesn't have family out here, but he had friends visiting in the hospital." Shawn had even gotten to meet a couple in passing.

"Apparently, some of them haven't handled his issues well." Lynn looked forlorn as she explained, "They've pulled away, haven't been around like they used to be. Those that are, well, Ethan keeps them at arm's length about things. He does the same to his family. He doesn't want them to worry about him being here alone."

The frown lines on his face only deepened. "Are you sure you should be telling me this?"

"Ethan had to sign a waiver to allow you to sit in. That allows us to discuss anything about his therapy details or things we've discussed in session." She leaned toward him, clasping her hands as she rested her forearms on her knee. "Ethan is at a crossroads right now. What you're suggesting with exposure therapy *could* send him backwards. But," she admitted with a slight sigh, "it could also be the breakthrough we need."

Shawn nodded in agreement. "I understand. Believe me; I don't want to do anything that could hurt him."

She gave him a knowing smile at that before becoming serious once more. "If it's going to work, then Ethan will need a strong support system. He needs people he can trust to guide him through this."

Shawn felt his gut clench as he thought about the implication. The idea of Ethan trusting him was flattering—made warmth spread through his chest unbidden. It also scared him, knowing that if he made a wrong step, then not only would that trust shatter, but he could literally shatter Ethan as well.

It was then Ethan decided to return. He looked a bit steadier on his feet, and Shawn couldn't help but give him an encouraging half smile. When it was returned, all Shawn could do was feel that warmth continue to grow, all the little doubts floating in the back of his mind being drowned out.

CHAPTER THREE

"Do you actually *stock* your fridge and cupboards?" Shawn groused, looking around at the contents.

"Not really." Ethan shrugged, observing from the other side of the counter. The small space was not ideal for the likes of Shawn—he'd been listening to Shawn complain as much for the past ten minutes. "I mostly get takeout or microwave meals."

Shawn pulled out a frozen pizza, eyeing it dubiously. "And those," Ethan added. He snickered when Shawn made a face and put it away.

"Clearly, I not only need to teach you to cook, but also to shop. At the very least you need to eat better. No idea how you stay in such good shape eating this junk." Shawn's head was in the fridge for a second look—as though it were somehow going to miraculously become better— and so he missed the blush crossing Ethan's face.

"Anything you can work with?" Ethan inquired to cover it up.

"I know I'm good, but I'm no miracle worker." He closed the door with a little force. "We're going on a shopping trip. Come on, kid. First lesson."

Ethan rolled his eyes. "Alright. But no more 'kid' crap."

Shawn grinned at him, ruffling his hair affectionately as they left the apartment.

* * *

Once they returned, Ethan's counters looked near to bursting. Despite the lack of space, somehow Shawn made it work. Granted, he grumbled the whole time, talking about the things he was missing.

"How do you not have a proper cutting board?" Shawn asked, looking at the small poly one with what amounted to disgust. He blew the dust off, raising a brow.

"I told ya. I don't really cook." Ethan didn't complain when Shawn asked him to wash the cutting board, before Shawn dug for the rest of the things he would need. Shawn handed off a colander containing the carrots and small red-skinned potatoes for Ethan to wash next.

With all the ingredients laid out in some sort of organized manner that only Shawn seemed to understand, he motioned for Ethan to join him. "So, while I prep the meat, can you cut all the vegetables?"

"Umm, sure." Ethan looked at the colander, the onion, and the bulb of garlic in hesitation. "How?"

"Just cut the carrots into chunks." Shawn reached past him for the garlic and broke off a few cloves to peel. "And those potatoes are small enough you can just cut them in fourths—half and half again."

Ethan's eyes widened a little as he watched Shawn mince the garlic with rapid speed. "We only need half the onion," Shawn continued, sliding the garlic into a little bowl and grabbing the onion to peel. "Think you can handle that?" The onion was cut in half, sitting on the board while Shawn put the other half into a zip-top bag and placed it in the fridge.

"Sure?"

Shawn gave him a little smile, clearly picking up on how lost he was. He took Ethan's hand in his as he pressed against Ethan's back. "Just slice it lengthwise like this." Shawn moved Ethan's hand for him, slicing through the onion a couple of times. "That thickness will work but doesn't have to be perfect." He patted Ethan's shoulder before moving away to tend to the meat.

Ethan had a hard time concentrating on his given tasks, trying to watch Shawn work. He moved with an easy confidence, trimming the fat off the small beef roast before adding all the spices, including the fresh garlic. Shawn took the onions, with a smile, dropping those and the beef into a pan to sear it.

"So who taught you to cook?" Ethan asked while cutting up the rest of the vegetables.

"The cook." Shawn gave a shrug when Ethan raised a brow. "Well, my parents certainly didn't cook. I was typically on my own a lot. Reading, doing work for school. One day I was in the kitchen and ended up watching. Became a new habit until the cook offered to show me things. Pretty soon I was helping out, and she was teaching me to cook for real.

"Eventually, my sister figured out where I was spending my time and joined us. It became a fun thing just for us." Shawn's smile was soft and filled with happiness.

"That's really nice," Ethan found himself replying. "My mom tried to teach Matty and me but..." Ethan lifted a shoulder. "Never really stuck."

"Clearly."

Ethan stuck his tongue out at him.

"It's not so bad though, is it?" Shawn checked.

Shawn transferred all the vegetables into the large pot, followed by the meat and all the juice. He had complained about not having the right equipment and that cooking the roast this way would just have to do. With a few more things added, Shawn dropped the lid on it and turned to look at Ethan.

Realizing he'd never answered, Ethan conceded, "I suppose not." After a moment, he ended up smiling. "Actually, it wasn't bad at all. We might have to do this again sometime."

Shawn's smile was worth it. "I would like that. I really would."

* * *

"Hey, Mom," Ethan greeted when Aileen answered the phone.

It was their usual time to talk, something they had set up when Ethan first left home for college so she could make sure to be home. The cell phone coverage was spotty on the ranch, and many places were outright blackout zones, so there was no counting on it. No, Ethan had to call on the good old-fashioned landline and hope she hadn't lost track of time doing chores or tending the garden.

"Ethan, hon, how are you?"

"Alright," he answered cryptically. He knew he wouldn't get away with it, yet tried anyway.

"Mm-hmm, and just how *alright* is 'alright'?"

"I dunno. Just good I guess."

"You haven't been missing your appointments with Doctor Bowers, have you?"

He let a little exasperation show in his voice. "No, Mom."

"And what did she have to say about you stopping that medication?"

"She was fine with it," he assured her. "She's letting me try some other stuff instead."

It wasn't the complete truth. Shawn had informed Ethan he'd passed along the reading material to Lynn and that she would look it over and make a decision before the next session. Ethan had talked some of the details over with Shawn already, though, and actually liked the idea of music therapy. Besides, he knew if anyone could convince her, it would be Shawn.

"More meds?" Aileen inquired.

"No, some different type of therapy. Has to do with music and keeping me calm."

"Like those meditation exercises you told me you started?"

"Yeah, like that. But it's something I can do while out in public. It should stop the panic attacks."

"Well, that's a good thing," Aileen encouraged. "If you both think it will work, then you should certainly give it a try." She let out a little sigh when she added, "It couldn't hurt at this point."

Ethan wasn't about to tell her that he was still capable of doing things to damage his progress. The looming idea of exposure therapy was proof of that. However, Ethan didn't want to worry her more than she already was. To that end, he remained as positive about things as possible, if only for her sake.

His father, Henry, was a facts kind of man. For good or ill, he wanted to know what the score was. Then he would be able to form a plan of attack to make things better if he could. In that, Ethan's talks with him were much more detailed when it came to the issues he was having. Ethan openly talked about how he had panicked and not been able to leave the house for three days, whereas to his mother, he would claim feeling under the weather.

Still, his parents both knew more than Matt did. As far as his little brother was concerned, Ethan's recovery had involved physical therapy, and that was all. Matt was completely unaware of his struggles with PTSD. It was Ethan who had insisted on it, knowing Matt would only worry unnecessarily for him.

It was hard enough looking into Matt's eyes after everything that had happened. He was Matt's hero—as cliché as that was—and to see Ethan broken had hurt Matt like Ethan never would have believed. No, knowing the scars Ethan bore were far more than just the physical would be even worse.

As Ethan had figured, his family was out on the range moving cattle when it happened. Spring was busy for them, watching over the new calves and bringing them all to safer grazing areas. Still, he had yet to be released from the hospital, when they showed up, having made the nine-hour trip in the old farm truck.

In all honesty, Ethan never expected to see his father. Henry was a good man, but the ranch was their livelihood, and leaving it unattended wasn't his style. Despite that, Henry wasn't about to not be there. He had almost lost one of his boys and had chosen to leave the ranch in the hands of neighbors for a bit.

Aileen stayed behind while Henry was forced to go back the day after Ethan's discharge. She mother-henned with no sign of stopping, but Ethan wasn't in a position to argue. He hurt on a good day, and his rehab to recover his strength left him drained.

While Aileen took care of the apartment and made sure he was eating, Matt was with him for moral support. He would help him to the bathroom or take him for laps inside the apartment to stretch his legs. Frankly, Ethan was glad he didn't have the energy to really go outside as it made him petrified.

It was, naturally, his mom who figured it out, long before Ethan came home from a meeting with his lieutenant to find he was temporarily suspended pending a psychological evaluation. It was Aileen who helped him find Lynn, all while Matt was out getting groceries, or sleeping when Ethan should have been but couldn't because of the nightmares.

The day they left for the airport in Seattle, two weeks after arriving, Matt wrapped his arms as gently as he could around Ethan's middle to give him a hug. "Love you, bro," Matt murmured.

Ethan choked on a mixture of emotion. Swallowing the lump in his throat as he turned his face into his brother's hair, he whispered back, "Love you too, Matty."

"Sure you won't come home for a little while?" Aileen asked, interrupting his wandering thoughts. It was an unfortunate habit since the shooting, his mind drifting as it did.

"Not just yet." He had been saying the same thing for months—ever since he'd been hurt, in fact. Aileen had wanted him to come home immediately, to finish his healing there. It was understandable, he supposed: a mother wanting to comfort her cub, to take care of and protect him.

As Ethan had been saying from the beginning, he had to stick it out, to do things on his own terms. He would fight this thing, and he would win. He couldn't do that by sequestering himself away at the ranch.

"As stubborn as your father," she grumbled.

It caused Ethan to smile. "An' that's why you love us both."

* * *

The Dining Car was buzzing with the late-afternoon lunch crowd. A classic American diner, it was housed within a vintage train car. The novelty was what got people through the door—the great food and service was what kept them coming back. As a regular, Shawn had a chocolate milkshake put in front of him right after he sat down.

Smiling up at the young waitress, he said, "Thanks, Mags."

She nodded with a bright smile of her own before looking over at Ethan. "What'll you have?" Ethan was eyeballing the shake, and Maggie chuckled. "Another shake coming up."

Ethan grinned over at Shawn before looking around some more. "I like it. Has a nice vibe to it." Glancing down at the small menu, he asked, "So any recommendations?"

"Bacon pancakes." Ethan raised a brow at that, and Shawn laughed. "What? You asked."

"Nothing wrong with bacon," Ethan relented. As he scanned the menu, he missed the way Shawn watched him instead.

Maggie returned with the second shake and clapped her hands together. "Usual?" she asked Shawn.

"'Course." When she addressed Ethan, he glanced at Shawn before asking for the bacon pancakes as well. "Good choice."

"When in Rome," Ethan offered, grinning around his straw as he tried the shake. "Wow...this is great." He took another long pull, making a humming noise of approval. Shawn loved the shakes; they were rich and creamy, just the way he preferred.

They made small talk while waiting, Ethan commenting on how he was only going to get more out of shape if he kept coming here, Shawn assuring him there was nothing wrong with his physique. Ethan blushed, and Shawn pretended not to see, quickly changing the topic.

* * *

Once their food arrived, Ethan felt himself salivating. A stack of pancakes with big pieces of bacon in them sat before him. "Wow" was all he could manage.

Shawn grinned, holding up the syrup that he'd just poured over his pancakes. "Warm maple syrup. Can't get much better than that."

More appreciative sounds left Ethan's mouth as he started to pour a generous helping of syrup over his own pancakes. After taking a rather large bite, he thought he would die right there. They were perfectly fluffy with crispy bacon mixed in the batter, providing a nice crunch. The syrup was the cherry on top. "Oh my God," he mumbled around a second mouthful. "This is perfect."

"Told you," Shawn replied. Ethan only grinned around his fork. Shawn shook his head, tucking into his own plate.

After a couple of minutes, Ethan sighed happily. He took a drink before his eyes found Shawn's. "Thanks for bringing me here," he said.

"My pleasure."

Ethan ducked his head as he added, "And for all your help. Really...you didn't have to." And that was the crux of it all. Shawn didn't owe him anything. They hadn't even known each other before that fateful night. Yet here Shawn was, doing more for him than any of his friends had—or been able to—brushing it off as no big deal. To Ethan, however, it was.

"I know." Shawn lifted a shoulder. "I want to." Letting it go with a nod, Ethan simply went back to eating, starting to swipe at his phone screen with his free hand.

They had come from the second session with Lynn. She had read the material Shawn sent her regarding the music therapy and given the go-ahead. Lynn was even more open to the exposure therapy this time around, saying that, if things went well with the music, they could talk about giving it the green light.

Ethan had started to make a playlist of music on the car ride over to the diner. The idea, as Lynn and Shawn explained it, was for him to pick music that inspired him. It was meant to calm him, to give him confidence. To that end, he was going through the music already on his phone and picking out what he thought would work.

It wasn't as though Ethan was completely against what Shawn was suggesting with the exposure therapy. He knew it was something he'd have to do eventually in order to get back to having a normal life. Well, as close to normal as one could ever get after experiencing trauma. Ethan simply wasn't as confident that he was ready to give it a go.

In all honesty, he was doing really well. He functioned normally in public, at his job. He was even alright with crowds—as much as he used to be anyway, since he'd always preferred to stay clear of congested spaces if he could. Ethan even had contact with police on occasion, as part of his new security work, and hadn't freaked out.

What bothered him was seeing cops en masse, whether it was at the scene of a call or simply hanging out somewhere. Of course, the game changed when he was already having an episode, much like the last incident that had prompted Shawn's rescue. There were days his anxiety acted up, sometimes for understandable reasons like nightmares, and others seemingly from nowhere. Those were the days that tested him, which he wanted to *fix*.

That was where Shawn's plan came in. The music was meant to keep him grounded and curb that anxiety. The goal was to help propel Ethan to the next step in his healing. Getting Ethan to walk through the doors of the precinct sounded crazy to his ears, but Shawn had only smiled and said that it would happen.

"How's it going?" Shawn inquired, nodding his head toward the phone and pulling Ethan from his thoughts.

Ethan gave a casual shrug. "I'm realizing I've got *far* too much music on this thing."

"No such thing." Shawn held out his hand. "Mind if I look?" Ethan just slid the phone across the table, taking a big slurp from his shake. Dragging his finger on the screen, Shawn took a look at the various songs. "You have way too much country."

"Pish. Whatever."

"Seriously, where's the jazz?"

"Never really listened to much of that," Ethan admitted. "I grew up with rock and country. And Ma always had easy listening on. Kids at school were listening to pop, and I had a Japanese roomie in college first year that got me into J-pop." He shrugged. "So, that's what I ended up with."

"Least there's no rap," Shawn grumbled. "I can listen to just about anything, but I drew the line on that in the bullpen."

Ethan laughed before assuring him, "Rap's not my thing, so no worries there."

"I must educate you in the fine art of jazz," Shawn concluded. He slid the phone back, conceding, "At least you have good taste in rock."

Ethan gave him a teasing grin. "Wouldn't have anything to do with it being all *old* stuff would it, *old man*?"

Shawn barked a laugh. "Yeah, well this *old man* still has plenty of tricks up his sleeve." He got up to go settle the bill, knocking Ethan in the shoulder with the back of his hand as he added, "Pup."

He missed the tender smile that settled onto Ethan's face, gaze trailing after him.

CHAPTER FOUR

"Keller! Zach!" Ethan held up his hand in greeting as they approached the pair of guys.

They were meeting in a relatively busy park, though Ethan had claimed they wouldn't be sticking around long. It had been said with a grin that made Shawn figure he should have asked more questions. Instead, he had simply gone with it when Ethan reached out and invited him along for a day out with his parkour buddies.

Both men were lean, the one introduced as Keller having a mess of brunet hair and freckles. Zach was one of the guys Shawn had met while visiting Ethan in the hospital. Today he wore a tank top and sport shorts that showed off his full-sleeve tattoos and the large dragon wrapping around his leg, his dark hair pulled back in a ponytail.

"'Sup, dude?" Zach greeted.

Shawn gave a little shrug as he looked around the park. "Just hanging out with Ethan today. Hope you don't mind I tagged along." As confident a person as he was, Shawn didn't do well with abrupt changes. He was completely out of his element—new place, new people, new situation. It wasn't like his job. This was a social environment, and he didn't really do *social*.

"Not at all," Keller assured him, grabbing his shoe as he brought his foot up to stretch. "We'll go easy on ya."

While Ethan was starting to stretch out, Zach asked, "So you parkour?"

Shawn held up his palms. "Just an observer." He wasn't about to admit he knew next to nothing about free running.

"Micah coming?" Ethan inquired, gratefully pulling the attention away from Shawn.

"Supposed to," Zach confirmed. "An' Becca."

"No Tanner?"

Shawn recalled meeting the college-aged kid as well when visiting Ethan one day.

"Big paper due," Keller explained. "And AJ's still a no-go for runs but he may show anyway."

"He busted his ankle on a landing," Ethan supplied.

"Yo!" someone called, everyone turning to find a tall, well-built black man jogging their way.

"Speak of the devil," Zach barked, pounding him on the back.

"Micah, Shawn," Ethan introduced casually.

Micah jerked his chin up at Shawn by way of greeting. "New rookie?" he inquired.

"Just watchin'," Ethan replied.

Like the others, Micah just accepted it, settling into the stretching and easy banter of the group.

Ethan bent over to touch the ground, folding practically in half. Shawn's brows rose, not even knowing the other man could do that. Ethan then pressed his palms flat to the ground and kicked his feet out. Just like that, Ethan was doing a handstand, his sweatpants sliding down to his knees, his T-shirt doing the same to his armpits, revealing a toned core—and the scar on his stomach.

Shawn's face must have been betraying his surprise as Ethan laughed up at him. "Dude, if you think this is impressive, you'll be shitting yourself before the day's out."

"Incoming," Keller warned, and Shawn turned to find a woman running their way. She leapt over a trash can, tucking and rolling before moving forward again with ease.

"Couldn't wait on us?" Micah joked.

"Can't help it you're a bunch of slowpokes," she replied with a smile, clearly already warmed up, given the light sweat already glistening on her skin.

She held out her hand to Shawn, introducing herself as Becca. She was a petite little thing with bright royal-blue hair. She had a wider frame but not overweight; Shawn figured a hobby like this one didn't allow for it, given all the calories they must burn.

"Not really dressed for a run are ya?" Becca mentioned to Shawn.

No, he wasn't. Shawn was wearing his normal attire while out of the office—a pair of designer jeans and plain tee layered over a long-sleeve shirt. "Tourist," Shawn remarked, nodding his head toward Ethan.

"He belongs to me," Ethan mentioned casually, unable to see the way Shawn's breath hitched in his chest. Shawn berated himself almost immediately, knowing that wasn't how Ethan had meant it. Rather Shawn attempted to play it cool as the group started to move.

Shawn wasn't expecting to be going to the nearby rooftops, but as soon as he stepped out onto the flat roof, he realized why. It was like a playground up there with multiple levels created by the different heights of the adjoining buildings and plenty of obstacles in the form of rails, ductwork, and the like. Still, the height worried Shawn, glancing over the edge to the ground five stories below.

"The realist in me feels the need to inform you this is dangerous," he mentioned when Ethan stepped up next to him. He met those deep-green eyes as he added, "And stupid."

Ethan gave him a bright grin. "That's half the fun."

Shawn figured pointing out the obvious that one slipup could mean death would fall on deaf ears and thus just hooked his thumbs in his pockets, leaning next to the stairwell door.

What followed was nothing short of impressive. Shawn watched them move seamlessly through the space. Whether running, jumping, rolling, or sliding, it all seemed to come so naturally. The fact they did everything without any kind of safety measures in place made it all the more amazing—and nerve-wracking.

Ethan flipped from one rooftop to the next that had a decent gap, plus a good five-foot drop, rolling through to his feet. Right behind him was Keller, tucking his legs up toward his chest as he leapt over the low array of pipes that Ethan had slid underneath moments before. Keller seemed to be taking turns shadowing the others in the group, copying their movements and taking it all in. He wasn't the most graceful, but he had the skill.

Coming from the opposite direction, Micah kicked his feet out in front of him to slide over the same set of pipes, although only his hands ever touched them. He then leapt at the wall, running up it and grasping at the edge before climbing up with relative ease. Waiting at the top was Becca who smirked before taking off—Micah hot on her heels—for a collection of ductwork that had been serving as Zach's jungle gym minutes before.

Zach was currently walking along a metal railing on the edge of the roof, nothing to stop him from falling except his own balance. "Normally we'd just keep going across the city until we couldn't run anymore," Zach informed him, hopping down when he got by Shawn. He stopped to swipe one of the water bottles Keller had hauled up to the roof with them.

As he was chugging the water, Shawn filled in, "But since I can't keep up with you..."

Zach lifted a shoulder and wiped the back of his hand over his mouth. "Not just that. Keller's still a rookie. We all want to be able to watch him. Harder to do when constantly on the move through a new space. Then you're just reacting, not planning."

"Can see why." The way they moved with such fluid ease, Shawn had no doubts that the four more experienced members of the group could act on a moment's notice as they ran. He watched Keller run up a wall, flipping off of it. "He looks like he's doing well enough."

"He's coming along. But we don't want any more accidents like AJ." Zach smirked. "Not that he was a rookie. Just a bad day. Could happen to any of us."

"Speak for yourself," Becca snarked, grabbing some water. "Yo!" she called to the others. "Come hydrate!"

"What you think?" Ethan asked Shawn as he joined them, smiling brightly.

Shawn couldn't help but grin right back. "I must say, I am very impressed." Ethan's smile only grew, throwing his head back and guzzling down his water as the others did.

"Y'know," Keller suggested, a little out of breath as he nudged Shawn's shoulder with his knuckles, "we should show you a few things."

"Oh no," Shawn argued instantly, throwing his hands up. "I don't think so."

"It'll be fun!"

"Yeah, dawg," Micah agreed. "You should try some stuff."

Ethan gave him a cheeky expression. "Might help ya catchin' criminals."

Shawn's brows rose. "That's what bullets are for."

As soon as the words left his mouth, Shawn could have kicked himself. His eyes widened, ignoring the laughter from everyone else, focus on Ethan. For his part, Ethan only flinched before shaking his head and joining in the laughter. "Ethan," he murmured all the same, stepping up into his space.

"Told ya, Greyson," he assured him, "I ain't made a glass." He slapped Shawn's shoulder roughly, lips twitching upward. "Come on. You can make it up to me by lettin' me teach ya a couple things."

Shawn caved, following Ethan without further argument.

* * *

"Where's your coffeemaker?" Ethan called from the kitchen.

When Shawn poked his head around the archway, his eyes were bugged out. "What is this blasphemy you speak of in my home?"

Ethan laughed loudly, the sound bouncing off the walls. "Oh come on. Seriously?"

"Yes, seriously." Shawn stepped into the kitchen, opening a cabinet overhead and pulling out a small canister. "I have tea if you'd like. Or there's water in the fridge. Maybe some pop left from last time my sister was over."

"Crossing my fingers for the pop." Ethan opened the refrigerator, rooting around. He was grateful to spot a can of Coke in the back. "I love your sister," he said, cracking it open as he nudged the door shut with his shoulder.

That was when he saw Shawn putting the kettle on the stove. While it was heating, Shawn turned his attention to a strainer ball, scooping in loose-leaf tea from the tin he'd taken down. "Wow," Ethan commented. "You're hardcore into this, aren't you?" He looked into the cupboard as Shawn returned the tin, finding over half a dozen in there. "Or you're addicted."

Shawn smirked, stifling a chuckle. "Davies would agree with you on that one." Ethan raised a brow in question, and he explained, "Another detective. He's a pain in my ass."

"Like him already." Ethan was smiling behind the Coke can, enjoying the unamused glance Shawn sent him. He could tell Shawn meant it in good humor, the quirk to his lips giving him away.

Since he was in the kitchen, Shawn pulled the roasting chicken out on the oven rack to check on it. "It's looking good," he mentioned, and Ethan had to bite back the sassy response of, *'That's not the only thing looking good.'* Honestly, where the hell had *that* thought come from?

As he watched Shawn move around, Ethan realized what the man had meant by *"needing his kitchen."* Working in Ethan's small space with limited ingredients was probably more taxing on Shawn than he'd let on. Ethan was glad to have agreed to the change in venue.

Ethan probably shouldn't have been surprised by how impressive the house was. It was an open layout, the living room able to be viewed from the kitchen through the large archway. A flat-screen TV hung above the fireplace, complete with a surround-sound system. The formal dining room at the entrance had been converted into a den with glass doors, though it wasn't really used, given the case files spread over the coffee table.

The kitchen was clearly where Shawn had spent his money remodeling the older home. There was a breakfast nook off it with large windows to allow the light in. It was all stainless-steel appliances: a pair of stacked ovens and a separate six-ring burner, the stars of the show. The countertops were gray-and-black granite, even the island, complemented by dark wood cabinets.

That really seemed to be the theme for the whole house, all warm woods and cool colors, with as much natural light as could be managed. Ethan couldn't deny he loved it.

"Why don't we go on the porch?" Shawn suggested with a little smile. Apparently choosing to forgo his tea, he pulled a bottle of wine from the built-in rack beside the pantry. "Be there in a minute."

Ethan ended up waiting in the open, sliding-glass doorway to the back patio. It was truly beautiful at Shawn's, and Ethan thought about telling him that their dinner dates would have to be moved there indefinitely. Blushing at his own thoughts of labeling their time together as *dates*, Ethan missed Shawn's approach.

Shawn held out a glass of red wine in offering, smiling softly. "Glad we could do this," he mentioned, leaning against the other side of the frame and peering into the backyard.

The way the sun twisted through the branches of the large trees was stunning and rather peaceful. Ethan could see why Shawn said he liked to spend so much time out there, simply reading.

"So am I," Ethan agreed. The last two nights they made plans had ended up a bust thanks to Shawn's caseload. Ethan figured Shawn's exhaustion—admitted or not—was the reason Shawn had insisted on hosting for once.

"Well, here's to more nights like this," Shawn said, holding his glass out in a toast. Ethan smiled, clinking their glasses together. His eyes were on Shawn, watching the curl of Shawn's lips behind his glass as they both took a drink.

The pair were silhouetted against the waning sunlight as they remained standing in the doorway, finding a shared peace in the comfortable silence.

CHAPTER FIVE

The music therapy was working. Ethan wasn't afraid to admit that Shawn had been onto something in that regard. Listening to his growing playlist on his phone was becoming the normal thing during his walk to work when the crowds were a bit thicker than usual. With earbuds in and music flowing through him, he was distracted from the otherwise constant barrage of stimuli.

What's more, whenever he felt himself starting to stress out, or even on the verge of panic, instead of hiding in the nearest bathroom stall, he grabbed his phone. It blocked out the noise while the music itself helped to soothe him. It refocused him in a way Ethan hadn't thought possible, like a key to being himself that he hadn't possessed before.

If Shawn had been right about that, then Ethan was willing to give him the benefit of the doubt when it came to the exposure therapy he was suggesting as well.

Ethan shouldered his messenger bag, which contained his laptop so he could work while at the station. He was standing at the back of Shawn's car, eyes sweeping nervously from side to side. In the underground parking garage, other officers were coming from their vehicles for shift change. None of them were particularly close though, having a section separate from the detectives and ranking officers.

"Okay?" Shawn checked, slipping his keys into his pocket and adjusting his soft leather satchel in hand. Ethan nodded, but Shawn seemed to already see the issues coming. "Go ahead and put your earbuds in. We just have a straight elevator ride up to the detectives' office."

Ethan gave him a thankful smile and did as advised. He already knew that it wasn't a large division, so there wouldn't be a lot of people to worry about. That was comforting, at least, knowing he could dip his toes into the water, as it were. It helped that they were detectives rather than uniformed officers, and having Shawn there as a lifeline didn't hurt either.

When they walked into the bullpen, there was already activity going on. Rather than the rush and flurry of a patrol room though, there was an ease of movement as people went about their work. It was unexpected but not unwelcome. Even so, Ethan stuck close to Shawn as they made their way across the room to the last row of desks.

Ethan shrugged off his bag, dropping it next to Shawn's desk as he looked around. They were near an office labeled as the captain's, the man in question sitting at his desk, on the phone. Shawn had mentioned needing Captain Sanchez's approval for Ethan to hang around. The former officer planned to thank Sanchez when he had the chance.

There was a tap on his shoulder, and Ethan took one of his earbuds out. "You can work on this side," Shawn directed. He cleared off a section, putting the stuff on the other side of the L-shaped desk, the computer sitting at the corner.

"Mornin', Greyson," a man greeted, stopping at the desk beside Shawn's to drop off a file before joining them. He held out his hand to Ethan. "You must be Brant."

Ethan nodded, taking his hand. "Ethan," he offered.

"Richard Davies."

The man looked like some sort of Viking, tall and lean with a shock of blond hair gelled into a coiffed mess. He wore a tasteful suit of high quality, complete with expensive leather shoes. Davies screamed of money, down to his chiseled jaw, great skin, and perfect teeth when he smiled.

Despite that, Davies didn't appear overtly arrogant about his station. There was a warmth to him, even if it was hidden by some sharp edges. The way Shawn told it, Davies's wit could shred skin.

"Thanks for letting me hang out," Ethan said. He knew from Shawn that as the senior detective, Davies had been a big decision-making factor for the captain. Sanchez had called them both into his office, asking Davies's opinion about having Ethan around a few days a week.

"No problem. Shawn says this will help, so I'm willing to back his play."

"Not as much of an asshole as he painted you to be," Ethan joked in turn.

Shawn snorted, peeling out of his trench coat to toss it across the filing cabinet. "Don't let him fool you. He's still a dick."

Davies nodded, hands in his pockets, as he said nonchalantly, "Oh, I am."

Alright, so a little arrogant. Ethan just smiled and shook his head. He could work with that.

"Now get the fuck away from my desk," Shawn snapped at his coworker. "I've got shit to do."

"Yes, Princess," Davies answered, giving him a theatrical bow. "Anything for you."

"Bite me," Shawn muttered in turn, dropping into his chair and booting up the computer.

Ethan couldn't help but laugh. Perhaps spending time at the station wasn't going to be half as bad as he'd figured.

* * *

Ethan grumbled as he got into the passenger seat. He looked a bit more haggard than usual, and Shawn was fairly certain it had nothing to do with the rain. "You okay?"

"Hmm?" Ethan was distracted with his bag a moment. "Oh, yeah. Well, no. My damn coffee machine broke, and I am *not* awake enough to deal with any of this shit." Shawn chuckled, shaking his head. "Hey, there's that coffee shop on the way to the station," he continued hopefully as Shawn pulled from the curb. "Could we stop really quick?"

Shawn didn't bother to hide his skeptical look but agreed all the same. It was hard not to when he got nailed with a perfected puppy look. He had to wonder if that expression worked on everyone, or if he was simply susceptible to it. As Ethan smiled and settled back into the seat, Shawn was willing to bet the former.

He waited in the car while Ethan darted inside, leaving Shawn to roll his eyes. He didn't understand the appeal of coffee, much less needing it to function in the mornings. If it was simply a caffeine thing, then there were certainly plenty of other options out there.

It was cause for many a spat between him and Davies in the bullpen. Even so, it was all in good humor rather than anything legitimately antagonistic. Shawn swore all the same that the next time the bastard tried to fuck with his tea, he would fill Davies's precious Corvette with seawater.

"Whew," Ethan remarked as he slid back into the passenger seat, "it's a zoo in there. Sorry for making you wait."

"No big deal." Shawn hadn't even noticed, instead being caught up in his own thoughts. "I don't get how the hell you all can be so addicted to that stuff." He crinkled his nose a bit.

"I went to Seattle U," Ethan pointed out. Naturally that explained everything—Seattle was well-known for having a coffee obsession. "On the ranch, it's typically just a cup to get the day started and maybe some if you're out on the plains at night to keep warm. But there? Yeah, coffee is life on that campus." Ethan was blowing on the steaming cup in his hands. "Want some?" he offered.

Ethan laughed so hard at Shawn's look of utter disgust that Shawn was surprised he didn't spill the whole cup. It was worth being noted that Ethan was gifted a new coffeepot a few days later.

* * *

It had been a couple of weeks since Ethan started coming to the station, and he'd managed to settle in nicely. He found an easy rapport with Davies. Even the other detectives had welcomed him, though they kept a respectful distance. Ethan figured Shawn's meaningful glare, if they hovered too long, had a lot to do with it.

That particular day, Shawn was so focused on his work that Ethan knew he wouldn't have eaten or drunk anything if he hadn't put it in front of Shawn. When he noted Shawn's mug was empty, Ethan sighed and took it, going to the small kitchenette area to get him more tea.

"He's still zoned?" Davies asked, fixing himself a cup of coffee. Having worked with Shawn for so many years, Davies was more than used to the man's habits. As Ethan got hot water from the countertop dispenser, Davies inquired, "Wanna snap him out of it?" The grin on Davies's face was wicked.

Ethan returned to the desk, finding Shawn combing through a report. Shawn grunted out his thanks when the mug slid into the corner of his vision, reaching for it blindly. He was so focused that he didn't even bother to look at it before bringing it to his lips.

When the hot liquid hit his tongue, Shawn spat it out in a spray. "What the fuck?" He crinkled his nose, finding coffee rather than tea in his mug. His eyes were wide, looking up at Ethan like he'd just kicked a puppy—total betrayal—and Ethan was hiding his mouth behind his hand, biting his tongue painfully to hold in a laugh.

Davies was literally howling. He was grasping onto the corner of his desk in an attempt to stay standing. "That was..." He sucked in a large amount of air to try again. "That was priceless. You should...see your face!" Davies was holding his side as it started to hurt from laughing too hard.

Ethan couldn't help it; he snorted out a laugh of his own. He schooled his features when Shawn's fiery eyes snapped back to him, clearly unamused, before Shawn's attention shifted to his coworker. "Davies," Shawn spoke, voice a mask of calm, despite gripping the handle of the mug so tight his knuckles turned white. "I swear I will make you regret that."

Davies didn't even blink, having zero sense of self-preservation. "I've been hearing the same shit for the last five years," he threw back. At least he had calmed down, no longer outright laughing even though his body was still vibrating.

"Yeah? Just remember that when your car gets towed," Shawn deadpanned. He stood then, grumbling, "Have to fix this mess," as he strode toward the kitchenette.

"Don't you dare touch my car!" Davies snapped, sobering instantly where his vintage Corvette was concerned.

Ethan shook his head, smiling in amusement as he inquired, "How often do you do that?"

Davies grinned, and it looked rather sharklike if Ethan was any judge. It wasn't a direct answer, of course, but Ethan got the idea. Instead Davies defended, "He's out of his zone, isn't he?"

"Fuck off," Shawn shot back, passing by with a tea bag steeping in his fresh cup.

"Eh, you'll get over it, Princess," Davies dug, scooping up a case file of his own. He smacked it against Ethan's shoulder and shared a conspiratorial smirk as he headed for the captain's office.

Ethan looked back at Shawn, who was muttering under his breath as he started to rearrange things on his desk—presumably to figure out where he'd left off. There was nothing for Ethan to do but attempt to hide his soft smile. It was better than admitting aloud that Shawn was rather adorable when his feathers were ruffled.

"What the hell were you so focused on anyway?" Ethan inquired, rounding the desk. He grabbed ahold of the back of Shawn's chair, leaning over him to gaze at the computer screen.

"Got curious about something."

Davies was returning then and snorted. "Yeah, and curiosity killed the cat."

Shawn's smile had teeth. "But satisfaction brought it back."

Ethan lowered his brows. "I've never heard that before."

Davies scoffed. "Don't get him started." He typed in his password before looking over at them. "Shawn's weird about all that kinda crap."

"It's not *crap*," Shawn argued. "It's actually really interesting." He turned the chair, smiling up at Ethan with what could only amount to excitement. "There's a lot of sayings we use that have completely changed over time. Mostly because pieces were chopped off."

"Like that damn tattoo you've got?" Davies pointed out, tapping away at his keyboard.

"Wait. *You* have a tattoo?" Ethan inquired, looking Shawn over head to toe in disbelief.

Shawn raised a brow. "And you don't?" Ethan shook his head. "Huh. Figured you would for some reason. I mean, given your friends and being a cop..." Shawn brushed it off. "Just the one," he ended up answering Ethan's original inquiry.

"Well, what is it?" Now Ethan was curious.

"It's a rib tattoo." Shawn tapped his left side. "Has the correct saying, 'The blood of the covenant is thicker than the water of the womb.'" He watched Ethan's lips as he repeated the phrase softly to himself. "A complete opposite of what people say today. Frankly, I prefer the original. Really spoke to me when I heard it."

"Take your shirt off, and show 'im, stud," Davies teased with a wink. Shawn flipped him off. "Hey now," he mock-complained, "that's inappropriate for the workplace."

"And a striptease is?"

"Your mind went there on its own," Davies answered with his hands thrown up, laughing. "I only said the shirt."

Despite blushing a little, Ethan commented, "I think Davies wanted to see."

"Seen it," he replied blandly, pretending to go back to work. "Not impressed."

"He likes bears," Shawn stated.

Without missing a beat, Davies threw back, "I like 'em with *boobs*."

Ethan barked out a laugh, both men joining him, before admitting, "Can't say I share the sentiment."

"Oh, I know."

Ethan raised a challenging brow.

"I've watched you check out just about every guy we have up here at least once." Davies smirked as he added, "Myself included."

It was Shawn who remarked, "Don't flatter yourself." After he took a sip of his tea, he griped about it not having enough sugar before heading back to the kitchenette once again.

Ethan watched him go, his mind wandering back to the tattoo. Admittedly, he was trying to picture how it looked on Shawn's skin, but it also posed a question or two.

Ethan went over and rested his hip against Davies's desk. "I'm guessin' Shawn ain't exactly close to his family." It had been a topic Ethan noticed Shawn didn't broach.

"Outside Sophia, not in the slightest."

"That's his older sister, right?" Shawn had mentioned her in passing a few times, mostly when they talked about Ethan's little brother. In truth, Ethan would have loved to meet her as she sounded like a really fun person.

"Yup. Pretty much the only one who ever gave a shit about him." Davies stopped typing to look up at him. "He comes from money. His folks were always too busy for them growing up. He doesn't associate with them unless Sophia twists his arm about it. Which is rare since he'll usually bitch about it to me. Can't say as I blame him... From what I gathered, they're real assholes."

Ethan nodded thoughtfully, looking up as Shawn returned. Naturally, Davies couldn't resist his usual brand of teasing. "Better, Princess?"

"Yes, darling," Shawn answered dryly in return, causing Ethan to chuckle.

Those two may have played animosity well, but Ethan could tell deep down they had each other's backs. That was par for the course in the law-enforcement community. Still, to have that tight of a bond was something special. Ethan was glad even someone as typically antisocial as Shawn could find that.

Noting that Shawn was already being absorbed back into his work, Ethan shook his head and pulled a chair up beside Davies's desk. Davies rose a brow at him in curiosity though didn't protest, rather, going back to looking at some crime scene photos.

"Does he always do this?"

Davies scoffed. "To call Greyson a workaholic is putting it mildly." He took a bite of an energy bar, talking around it. "I'm the senior detective 'cause I've got more years than Shawn does. He also doesn't want the job. Would rather be solving cases than dealing with the extra duties." Davies shrugged, taking another bite. "But at the same time, the bastard works more hours than even I do. Least he could get the pay increase."

Ethan rolled his eyes, looking over at Shawn as he commented, "Would be nice for him to get a night off every once and awhile. Maybe I could talk him into taking off early."

"Good luck with that."

Ethan looked back at Davies, but he was skimming over a report. "I've tried but nothing short of a threat seems to work." Once more he received Davies's full attention. "Even if you get him out of here, I guarantee he'll be back later."

"We'll see." Ethan took it as a personal challenge.

He wandered over to Shawn's desk, acting casual. "Hey, it's getting pretty late. You wanna go grab a bite to eat? Or we can go back to my place and order takeout."

Shawn rubbed at his eyes and yawned, checking the time for himself. "I think I'll have to give you a rain check. I should probably go home and sleep. I'll take you home though if you're ready."

As Shawn was gathering his stuff, Ethan looked over at Davies, who gave him an impressed nod. Still, Ethan had to wonder if Shawn was being entirely honest with him about where he was headed after dropping Ethan at his apartment.

Sure enough, about twenty minutes after Ethan got settled, his phone beeped with a text from Davies: *He's back.*

CHAPTER SIX

On the back porch, the sun was shining in with a low glow, the harsh rays cut up into streams by the trees in the yard. The array of colored glass and wind chimes that Shawn had gathered over the years—either on his own or through his sister—were catching the light and bending it, the chimes *tinkling* lightly with the intermittent breeze. In a cleared section of the porch, Ethan was sitting cross-legged, hands resting on his knees, eyes closed as he breathed slowly and steadily.

Shawn was careful to tread softly so as not to disturb him. He placed a cup of tea on the stand near Ethan before settling on a wicker chair. He blew on his own tea, eyes on Ethan. The man seemed peaceful now that he'd finally been able to settle into his meditation.

Shawn hadn't thought him the type to meditate. In truth, Ethan wasn't. It was something Lynn had suggested in order to help with his treatment. However, Ethan found it difficult to get in the proper mindset, to relax enough to settle into a state of total peace. According to Ethan, he wasn't even sure he was doing it right, though apparently, it was much easier to set himself at ease in the quiet of Shawn's porch than at his apartment.

Shawn couldn't exactly blame him; the building Ethan lived in was full of activity. The few times Ethan had been over to the house to try to meditate, Shawn had seen how any sudden noise would jar him immediately. No doubt Ethan was frustrated by trying to do something that involved being so still with all the distraction of the apartment.

Sipping at his tea, Shawn observed Ethan and couldn't help but smile. Ethan looked perfectly content, the picture of calm.

It was a nice day, and they both had the time off. Shawn figured Ethan would have gone out with those crazy parkour friends rather than be cooped up with him. Yet when Shawn opened the door around noon, there Ethan was with takeout in hand and a smile on his face.

"Free for the day?" Ethan inquired, passing over a burrito from the bag he set on the table.

"Was thinking of sitting outside and catching up on my reading."

Ethan nodded, taking a healthy bite of his own taco. "Mind if I join ya?" he asked with his mouth full.

Shawn resisted the urge to comment on the bad manners, instead giving a shrug. "You're always welcome here."

Ethan's bright smile was worth it.

Shawn put his feet up, leaning back after trading his tea for his book. Unfortunately, the novel he had been so engrossed in before Ethan's arrival couldn't seem to compete with said man's presence. Shawn found himself rereading the same paragraph three times before finally giving up with a sigh.

He looked over at Ethan, still at ease, and held back from tossing the book onto the coffee table in frustration. Shawn didn't want to interrupt his meditating, especially when Ethan seemed to have finally gotten into it. Shawn figured Ethan hadn't had much of a safe headspace since the shooting.

Shawn frowned, forced to remember how they had gotten to this point in the first place. Then again, he supposed it wasn't *all* bad, given it had brought him such a close companion.

"Hey," Ethan greeted with a smile. Shawn had come by the hospital right after work to check in on him. "Wasn't expectin' to see you again."

"Told you I would be back." He pulled a chair up to Ethan's bedside where he had been the night before. "How do you feel?"

"Well, they keep feeding me morphine, sooo pretty good all things considered."

Shawn couldn't help but laugh. "Nothing wrong with a little positivity."

"Damn straight." Ethan's grin was a bit lopsided, but at least his words weren't slurred. Therefore he was certainly lucid enough.

"Were they able to get ahold of anyone for you?"

Ethan frowned and gave a shrug. "It's spring," he said by way of explanation. When Shawn only gave him a curious look, Ethan expanded, "My family owns a ranch. Calving season we're always out on the range moving the herd to a safer area. It's spotty reception at best."

"Oh." Shawn wasn't sure what to say to that. It was unfortunate that his family couldn't be with Ethan in this situation; however, it wasn't as though it was their fault either. Shawn couldn't say he knew what

that felt like. "No extended family you could call instead?" Shawn tried. "Maybe someone who can get out to them?"

Ethan waved it off. "No other family in the picture. Just my folks and my little brother, Matty." He shrugged. "They're all out there. And any of the neighbors would be busy doin' the same thing. Spring's a busy time back home."

"Well then, how 'bout a girlfriend or something?" Ethan had to have someone to be with him.

Ethan barked out a laugh. "Yeah, no." He cleared his throat. "No, I'm gay. But, uh, before you ask, no, no boyfriend either."

"Ah." Well, Shawn had really put his foot in his mouth that time.

Ethan must have taken his lack of comment wrong as he mentioned, "If that's a problem…"

"What? Oh, no, no not at all. I'm bi, so it's…it's fine." He could feel heat on his cheeks. It wasn't as though Shawn was embarrassed by his sexuality; he had long ago stopped being apologetic over it. It was just he was never particularly blunt about the matter.

"Cool" was all Ethan had to say on the subject, settling back against the pillows.

Relaxing into his own chair, Shawn stated, "Well, since no one else is going to hang around, guess you're stuck with me."

Ethan chuckled again, shaking his head. "I got friends, ya know." When Shawn looked around pointedly, it earned him a fuller laugh and a muttered, "Fuck you, man."

Shawn grinned at him. Deciding to change the topic, he asked, "So where's home?"

Ethan's face lit up as he started to tell Shawn about the ranch in a small town south of Missoula.

* * *

"You look well," Lynn greeted as they stepped into her office.

It was true. Ethan had a sort of glow to him. "Feelin' good," he confirmed.

"How about you, Shawn?" she asked, obviously noting he himself was a bit more haggard than usual.

"Sleeping for a couple days sounds good to me," Shawn answered dismissively. Sure, there was more than that floating around in his head, but he didn't want to get into it.

Seeming to sense this, Lynn asked Ethan how things were going as they settled into their usual places. Although, this time it was Shawn leaning into the corner of the couch dejectedly. He may as well have worn a sign that said *"Psychoanalyze me."*

"It's been great," Ethan said, giving her a genuine smile. "No anxiety, no panic attacks. Was a little nervous the first day. But Shawn had me listen to my music, and it was all fine."

Lynn was obviously pleased. "That's wonderful. I'm very relieved to hear it." She looked at Shawn as she asked, "What do you think, Shawn?"

"He's been good," he agreed.

She frowned. "Usually you're more talkative than this. Is something wrong?"

"Just some stuff I'm working through." He gave her a little shrug, looking away from those all-too-knowing eyes. Of course he ended up looking right at Ethan, who was now appearing concerned. With a sigh, Shawn averted his gaze once more.

"If you want to talk about it—"

"I'd prefer to keep things about Ethan," he interrupted, perhaps a bit too quickly. To cover, Shawn added, "This is supposed to be his time, after all."

Lynn nodded, compelled to offer, "If you'd like, I'd be happy to talk to you privately afterward."

"I don't think that will be necessary, but thank you." Shawn honestly thought he deserved a medal for being so nice about it. It was all he was able to do to act natural in their previous sessions. Granted, Shawn had managed because it had been about Ethan, not him.

"If you ever need to, the offer will stand."

He was thankful when Ethan came to his rescue. "So I was thinking about going down to the patrol room this week. Maybe talk with some of the guys I used to work with."

Shawn relaxed back against the cushions, letting out a slow breath. He hadn't realized how tense Lynn's prodding had made him.

Even being out of sorts, Shawn was paying attention. He had the sneaking suspicion that Ethan was bluffing. Ethan had no intentions of doing what he suggested. No, he was trying to shield Shawn, the way Shawn had been shielding him. That was certainly different.

* * *

"What's up with you?" Davies inquired when he entered the kitchenette, slapping Shawn on the shoulder. "You seem off."

Shawn turned to lean back against the counter as his tea began steeping while Davies made up his coffee. "Had another therapy session with Ethan."

"Yeah? He doing okay since he's been coming here?"

"He's fine," Shawn assured him. "Lynn's happy with his progress and so's he."

"So what's the problem?"

"Had some flashbacks of my own the other day. Messed me up a little, I guess, and she saw that. Offered to 'talk me through it.'"

"Ahh, and you don't do therapists." Davies nodded in understanding as all the pieces fell into place. Shawn had a well-known aversion to the "Department Shrink," causing a fuss whenever he was required to see the man after an incident.

"Exactly."

Davies mimicked Shawn's stance, holding his mug as he stirred the contents. "And why is that?"

Shawn sighed, glancing over at him briefly before looking down at his feet. If Davies had asked him the same thing just last year, Shawn would have refused an explanation instantly. However, Davies had come to earn his trust, had proven that despite being a pain in the ass, he was also a good guy. The question was whether he could confide to Davies something that so few people even knew about.

Another pair of detectives came and went before Shawn finally decided on his answer. He turned to fix his tea as he explained, "My parents put me in conversion therapy." Out of the corner of his eye, he saw Davies tense. "It didn't last long. Never went off to one of those *camps* or anything. Just one-on-one sessions."

"Fuck," Davies growled under his breath. His pale eyes were narrowed with intent. "How could those bastards do that? How old were you?"

"Fourteen." He sighed, taking a drink of his tea. "I didn't exactly come out as bisexual willingly. I knew what their reaction would be. My sister was the only one who knew."

"So how'd they find out?" Davies shifted a little closer in what was clearly supposed to be a comforting manner, and Shawn appreciated it. Talking about his family was never easy as too many bad memories lingered in the recesses of his mind.

"They were supposed to be out of town for a few more days." He managed to look at Davies as he admitted, "They caught me and my boyfriend in the pool."

"Oh, please don't tell me—"

"We were just making out." Shawn leaned closer and knocked their shoulders together, managing a slight smile at Davies who mirrored the expression. "But, as you can imagine, they freaked the hell out."

Davies nodded, both of them sipping at their drinks as another detective slipped in to grab something. Once she was gone, Davies continued, "But that's not the real problem here. You said you weren't doing well *before* goin' to the doc's. So what's got you all...?" Davies made a circular motion with his hand that was supposed to encompass Shawn.

Softly he replied, "Was thinking about that night Ethan was shot and...started thinking about Austin."

Davies heaved a sigh, shaking his head. "Shawn, you can't still be blaming yourself for that."

"I'm not. Just...brought up a lot of bad memories."

Shawn's former partner from when he was a patrol officer, Austin, had been killed while on duty. Remembering Ethan bleeding out brought it all to the forefront. Shawn had already had one man die in his arms, and he'd been determined not to let Ethan be next. His blood had been on Shawn's hands.

Whereas he couldn't save Austin, he *had* saved Ethan. It had started out as feeling responsible for Ethan, making sure he was alright. Except, it had started to grow into much more than that.

"*And*?" Davies prompted as though reading his mind.

"You know it's not fair to use your deductive-reasoning skills on colleagues," Shawn pointed out.

"Not a colleague. A friend."

Shawn glanced over at him, lips quirked into a smile. He looked away as he admitted, "Made me realize I'm having feelings about Ethan."

"God, anyone could see that a mile away." Shawn's head snapped to him again, Davies smiling into his coffee cup as he took a drink. "Hell, he makes goo-goo eyes right back. Honestly figured you two were already...you know."

Shaking his head in disbelief, Shawn argued, "Ethan just sees me as a friend."

Davies scoffed in return. "For a detective, sometimes your observation skills need a little work."

Shawn's brows lowered, and he frowned at Davies when he headed back out to the bullpen. Ethan couldn't actually think of him romantically, could he?

Chapter Seven

Ethan walked through the doors of the detective unit, gaze wandering around the already bustling office. He nodded to a couple of the guys as he passed by. When he caught sight of Shawn's desk, Ethan sighed and shook his head.

Shawn was leaning forward, head pillowed on his folded arms. His face was hidden from view, but given the deep breathing and mussed hair, Ethan was willing to bet he'd fallen asleep. He ran a hand along Shawn's spine, a steady pressure as he started to rub. Bending forward, Ethan pitched his voice low. "Shawn… Hey, Shawn, wake up."

Shawn stirred, giving a protesting moan. It caused Ethan's lips to quirk. Unable to help himself, his hand carded through soft strawberry-blond curls. "Shawn, time to get up," he insisted gently.

"Mmm, find someone else to do it," he complained, though it came out slurred with sleep. "'M busy." Ethan chuckled, drawing Shawn's attention and pulling him back to consciousness. Shawn sat up with a groan, rubbing his eyes and looking up at Ethan. He blinked a few times before being able to focus. "Ethan? Wha–?"

"Morning" was his amused reply. He'd never seen this side of Shawn before, and it was rather endearing.

Shawn looked around, noting his current surroundings. He was no doubt wondering what he'd been doing. "What time is it?" he grumbled, looking at his watch. His gaze snapped up to Ethan again. "How did you get here?"

Ethan shrugged, leaning a hip against the desk. "Caught a cab. Figured you might have gotten called out to a case or something." He had planned to be there whenever Shawn got back.

Groaning again, Shawn ran his hands over his face and cursed softly. "I'm sorry. Didn't mean to leave you hanging."

"Hey, there's no need to apologize." Ethan frowned down at him, taking in his disheveled appearance. "You've been here all night."

"Certainly wasn't the plan." Shawn pressed a hand to his lower back, bowing it to try to work the kinks out. "Damn case is pissing me off." Something popped, and Shawn melted with a sigh.

"Come on," Ethan prompted, holding out his hand. When Shawn only looked at him, Ethan wiggled his fingers. Shawn accepted the offer, Ethan pulling him to his feet. "Let's go get you fed and into a bed."

"I can't," he argued immediately, brows dropping. "The case—"

"Can wait." Ethan took a deep breath, gazing at him with undeniable fondness. "Let's go. Looking with fresh eyes can only help."

Shawn begrudgingly agreed. "Pushy bastard," he muttered all the same, Ethan smirking behind his back.

* * *

As Shawn was gathering the needed files into his satchel, something suddenly occurred to him now that he was awake enough to think straight. His eyes widened, looking over to meet Ethan's gaze. "You walked all the way in here on your own."

Ethan blinked, and after a long moment, a slow grin spread across his face. "Yeah. You're right."

Pride swelled in Shawn's chest. Without even thinking about it, he wrapped his arms around Ethan's shoulders and pulled him into a hug. Shawn wasn't just impressed that Ethan had managed to walk by all those uniformed officers to get up there. It was the fact that Ethan had done it all for *him* that really floored Shawn.

Ethan patted his back when they separated, his arm sliding around Shawn's shoulder as Ethan grabbed the satchel with his free hand. "Come on, detective," he mused. "Let me drive you home."

Shawn didn't fight him, barely even registering going into the parking garage or Ethan pilfering his keys. He was fairly certain he'd dozed off during the ride, not really coming around until the engine was cut, and his temporary chauffeur prodded his shoulder.

When Ethan said he'd take him home, Shawn just assumed it would be to his house, not Ethan's apartment. Still, there was no sense in arguing, and really, Shawn found he didn't mind the chosen destination at all.

He allowed himself to lean on Ethan a bit in the elevator, completely willing to admit he had really burned himself out this time. Not that it was anything new, which, of course, was part of the problem. There was no way Shawn would concede defeat or call it quits, but afterward he could sure berate himself for it.

"Sorry about all this," Shawn mentioned.

Ethan smiled softly over at him, arm coming around his back in support, encouraging Shawn to lean on him more as they made their way down the hall. "Don't worry about it. Lemme take care of *you* for once." Busy unlocking his door, Ethan missed the way Shawn's cheeks reddened.

Admittedly, the idea of someone taking care of him had never been an appealing concept. Shawn didn't like to feel weak or be a burden. Somehow Ethan being the one to offer didn't make him feel like that in the least. If anything, Shawn felt like he could finally take the chance to *breathe,* and the world wouldn't fall to pieces around him while he did so.

"Wanna take a shower before you sleep?" Ethan asked, hustling him inside.

"I think passing out sounds about right," he admitted, making Ethan smile.

Ethan took Shawn back to his room. Grabbing a pair of soft, worn pajama pants, he offered them to Shawn along with a T-shirt. "Thanks," Shawn said with a yawn.

"No problem. Get some rest." Ethan smirked as he added, "I'd say sleep as long as you want, but I know better, so I'll wake you for lunch, okay?"

The corner of Shawn's mouth quirked up. "Sounds good."

"I'll be here if you need anything." Ethan reached out and rubbed Shawn's arm from shoulder to elbow, up and down a few times. Shawn fought the urge to return the gesture—or offer anything more intimate. "Sleep tight," Ethan said, taking his leave so Shawn could get some proper rest.

* * *

A few hours later, Shawn padded out into the living room, still in his borrowed clothes. He hadn't been expecting to find Ethan poring over his case files, cup of coffee in hand. It clearly hadn't been the man's first cup either if the way he fidgeted was anything to go by.

"Hey," Shawn greeted, drawing his attention.

"Oh, you're up." Ethan looked distractedly toward the clock on the cable box. "I was gonna let you sleep some more."

Shawn gave a little shrug before letting out a yawn as he stretched up onto his toes, arms reaching up. "Honestly, I feel a lot better now."

"That's good." Ethan offered him a smile. He followed Shawn's gaze to his files and quickly tried to apologize. "I know I shouldn't have. I'm not on the force anymore. But I thought I might be able to help and—"

"Relax." Shawn sat next to him. "I don't mind." Ethan nodded slowly, refusing to look at him. Attempting to ease the tension, Shawn prompted, "Didn't you say something about making me lunch?"

Ethan smiled softly at him in thanks. "Sure. I'll go whip something up for us."

As Ethan went into the nook, which barely passed for a kitchen in Shawn's opinion, Shawn called, "You have a fire extinguisher, right?"

"Oh, har, har. You shoulda been a comic."

Shawn smirked, playing along. "Well, I'm pretty enough for movies."

"That you are," Ethan agreed easily. Ethan's back was to him, so he missed the blush that crawled to the tips of Shawn's ears. He was grateful that Ethan didn't question the end of their playful banter, already too absorbed in finding something to make to notice the lull in conversation.

Rather than focus on the implication behind Ethan's words, Shawn put his deductive-reasoning skills to other uses. He had already become fully absorbed in his case files once more when something was thrust under his nose.

"A sandwich?" Shawn mused, accepting the plate. "I make you home-cooked meals, and I get a sandwich?" He raised a teasing brow at Ethan as he sat next to him.

"Well, as you pointed out, I don't have a fire extinguisher. And I didn't feel like attempting to burn down the building today."

Shawn chuckled, holding up half of his sandwich in a toast. Ethan tapped their sandwiches together, and then dug in with as much enthusiasm as he ever showed one of Shawn's meals. It was one mystery solved at least. Ethan just loved food, plain and simple.

"We need to talk about all the junk you eat," Shawn mentioned before taking a bite of the turkey sandwich he'd been served.

"Not all of us can be amazing cooks, y'know." Ethan wiped a bit of mayo off his chin.

"I like to think I've taught you a thing or two, though. Certainly you can take a little better care of yourself."

Ethan waved him off. "So I have a theory," he began, moving aside some papers before tapping the one he wanted. It was a picture of the crime scene, specifically the victim. "Now most crimes are motivated by love or money. Or both."

"She didn't have anything of real value," Shawn remarked. He'd gone through the photos and inventory of the apartment, as well as the report that looked into her financials. There were no hidden caches of money or priceless heirlooms.

"Nothing was missing," Ethan conceded. "No signs of the place being gone through. So that leaves the love angle."

"According to all the statements" —Shawn began, attempting to find them in the mess of paperwork one-handed— "she wasn't seeing anyone."

"I read that too," Ethan assured him, "but here's the thing..." He tapped the photo of the victim again. "See her finger? She was in a relationship recently, and from the looks of things, it was serious."

Shawn noticed the tan line on the woman's ring finger then and shook his head. "I completely missed that." He really *had* been staring at everything too long.

"My money's on the guy across the hall." Ethan flipped through a stack of statements before finding the one he wanted and pulling it out to place in front of Shawn. "If he isn't the ex himself, then he knows who is."

Shawn scanned the statement and shook his head. "He claims he barely knew her, and he hadn't seen any boyfriends or the like."

"And you believe that?" Ethan asked skeptically.

"I didn't do the interview. It's Ronnie's case. I caught it when she caught pneumonia." He swore the woman always had the worst timing to get sick. "Hell, she didn't even handle the statements herself. She had the officers on scene do it while she dealt with the coroner and CSIs." It wasn't an unusual practice, especially with a large area to canvas.

"Well lemme tell you," Ethan replied in amusement, "when you live in an apartment building, you know shit about your neighbors you don't wanna know. Even if you barely talk and basically know nothing about them? You still know their business. There's *no way* this guy lived across the hall from her and didn't know her comings and goings."

Shawn followed the line of logic. "So he's either the ex in question...or he's jealous of her other relationships."

"Or both. He sees some other dude hanging around, confronts her, and things go bad." Ethan shrugged. "Or maybe he wanted her back. Hell, maybe he knows the dude that did it and is covering for 'im. Whatever the case, he knows more than he said."

"You are a genius," Shawn concluded, looking over at Ethan. His big, dopey grin made an answering smile cross Shawn's face. There was no helping it, Shawn was so filled with excitement that he grabbed ahold of Ethan, dragging him to his side.

"Well, I *am* good," Ethan agreed, leaning against him, his arm slipping around Shawn's back, head resting on Shawn's shoulder momentarily.

Shawn turned his face in toward Ethan at the same time Ethan looked up. They both froze, trading the same air as their lips hovered closely together. It would be nothing to cross that little space, to press their mouths together in a kiss.

Eyes widening at his dangerous thoughts, Shawn drew back, watching as Ethan looked away just as quickly. With Ethan's face cast in shadow, it was hard to tell, but it appeared as though he was blushing. Shawn bit his lip, not wanting to think about what that could mean.

"I, uh..." Shawn cleared his throat, looking at the clock on the DVR. "I should get back to the station." He tapped the file. "Follow up on this."

"Yeah." Ethan nodded, putting a little more conviction in his voice as he repeated, "Yeah."

Shawn stood, and retreated to the bedroom to change quickly. When he returned to gather up all his files, he found Ethan hadn't moved. "Thanks again for your help." He paused when Ethan looked up at him, a question in those green eyes.

Unfortunately, Shawn didn't have answers to give him and thus told him, "I'll talk to you later," before snagging his trench coat from the hook by the door and practically fleeing.

It wasn't until Shawn slipped into his car that he realized how close he had been to losing control and kissing Ethan. He sighed, resting his head against the steering wheel for a long minute. Shawn cursed himself as a coward as he started the car and put it in gear.

CHAPTER EIGHT

"I was beginning to think you died" was the greeting Ethan received when Skype connected. The man, only a few years his senior, gave him a cheeky grin.

"Can't help it you're always so damn busy," Ethan shot back, not hiding his own smile. It was all in good fun.

"Yes, well, being a Feeb will do that."

Ethan chuckled and shook his head. "How ya been, Sebby?"

Sebastian cringed at the horrid nickname. "Y'know, the usual. Getting shot at, beating the crap outta people, and generally abusing my power."

Laughing, Ethan replied, "Sounds about right."

"How about you, *ka ¢a*?" The tribal word for brother rolled off Sebastian's tongue, one of many Kootenai phrases Ethan had been taught over the years, although he was far from fluent.

"Been better," Ethan admitted, face falling and revealing just how tired he truly was.

"What's goin' on?"

"I, uh, I may have almost kissed Shawn." Ethan could feel the heat on his cheeks as he ducked his head.

"Your detective?" Sebastian asked. A huge grin split his face then. "Well it's about damn time. Thought the pining was gonna do me in."

"Pining?" Ethan raised a brow. "Seriously?" Sure, he'd told his best friend about Shawn, about how Shawn was helping him with therapy and whatnot. But *pining*?

"Uh, did ya hear the way you talked about him?" Sebastian shot back. "*Pining.*"

Ethan scoffed. Not that he could say anything as they teased each other mercilessly at all times. It was an easy rhythm they had fallen into since they had first met back in college. In fact, it had been Sebastian who had convinced him to go into law enforcement.

Before Ethan could reply, his friend forged ahead. "And don't change the subject. You said *almost* kissed him. Details?"

Ethan groaned, rubbing his hands over his face. "I made a total fool of myself."

"Doubtful."

It was all Ethan had been able to think about since Shawn had left. He'd spent the afternoon waiting impatiently for Sebastian to get home so they could chat. As anxious as he was, Ethan would have been tempted to drive the rough hour or so down to Seattle where his best friend worked if he had a car to do so.

"So I found him asleep at his desk this morning," Ethan began, explaining how he had dragged Shawn home and then later helped him with a potential break in the case. "I may have snuggled up to him when he put his arm around me and then..."

Ethan could still feel the heat of Shawn's body against him, the breath on his face. It made his heart beat faster with the memory.

"Shoulda gone for it, man," Sebastian insisted.

"Dunno he feels the same," Ethan replied softly.

"Bullshit." Sebastian snorted, brushing his mess of dark curls from honey eyes. "Look at what he just did. He *obviously* cares about you!"

"As a friend, yeah, but as more than that?"

Sighing, Sebastian put his chin in his hand. "You are impossible."

Ethan licked his lips, looking down at his hands. Sure, he could admit falling for Shawn somewhere along the way—although he drew the line at *pining* as Sebastian claimed. *Could Shawn really feel the same?*

Thinking back, it wasn't as though that was the first time they'd touched. There were plenty of cases of more-than-casual physical contact. Before, Ethan had brushed off the lingering glances he caught, or the shy little smiles. Now they all seemed to make sense.

"Is he dating anybody right now?" Sebastian interrupted his thoughts.

"No, he spends all his time with..." Ethan looked up, realizing the words that were coming from his mouth. "Me."

Sebastian gave him a smug grin.

* * *

Seated on his back porch, Shawn was enjoying the afternoon with a cup of tea. He was ordered by the captain to take a few days off after the stunt with him falling asleep at his desk. He'd been allowed to brief

Davies over the new angle to work, thanks to Ethan, and then not so subtly told to *"Get the fuck home."*

In all honesty, he needed the rest. He always did these things to himself, running himself into the ground until someone forced him to stop and take a break. Just getting a solid night's rest, able to sleep in and have a late brunch, was doing wonders for his psyche.

With the case behind him and now fully recharged, that meant his mind was free to wander. Naturally that meant he was thinking about the close encounter at Ethan's apartment the day before. Shawn heaved a sigh, taking a sip of his new white tea; he knew the hot liquid wasn't the main cause of the warmth in his chest.

They had been so close to sharing a kiss; Shawn wasn't going to lie about that. Really, he could have kicked himself for being so blind. Everything they had gone through, the time they'd been spending together; it had been obvious they had gotten close. It wasn't until that moment that Shawn realized exactly *how* close.

There was no denying he was attracted to Ethan. Hell, who wouldn't be? Ethan was gorgeous, and what's more, he had a wonderful soul. Shawn scoffed at his existential musings, but they were undoubtedly true. Somewhere along the line, he'd fallen for Ethan. The question was what to do about it.

He was fairly certain Ethan felt the same, his reaction to their proximity telling in and of itself. Still, if Shawn read the situation wrong, then he could potentially be ruining what had become a really good friendship—even if Davies had insisted upon the fact.

Shawn continued to mull over the situation until he ran out of tea. After he put the kettle on to make more, he took a deep breath and decided on a course of action.

He pulled out his phone, then hitting the speed dial that connected him to Ethan's cell. Ethan answered after a few rings with a bright greeting. Encouraged by that, Shawn smiled. "Hey, gotta question for you. Think we can go out for dinner on Friday?"

"Go out?" Ethan repeated, and Shawn could practically hear the gears spinning.

"Yeah, with this caseload, I've just been completely wiped," he replied casually. "So I was hoping we could have someone else cook for us instead." It was as good an excuse as any and saved Shawn from having to call it a date. That way, if he was completely off point, there would be no harm done.

Shawn really hoped that wasn't the case. The more the thought crystallized in his mind, the more he found he liked the idea.

"Sure, that's fine," Ethan answered. "Did you have a place in mind?"

"Yeah, I'll pick you up."

"Given yer tastes, I'm guessin' I'm gonna have to dress up." He could hear the teasing in Ethan's tone and smiled softly.

"Something dress casual is fine," Shawn assured him.

"Dress casual?"

Shawn had to chuckle at the other man's confusion. "Nice pants and shirt. Nothing fancy."

"Alright then." Ethan didn't seem too sure, but he went with it.

Cutting him a break, Shawn turned the conversation. "Thanks again for the help yesterday. Sorry I didn't call sooner."

"No, no, it's alright. No problem, dude."

"Still...the legwork with Davies, and then he kicked me out to do the rest on his own. So I'm on a forced minivacation the next few days."

"Yeah, we'll see how long that lasts."

"Hey now," Shawn defended with a little laugh.

"We both know you'll be back tomorrow. If you make it a whole second day, I'll be shocked."

"Yeah, yeah..." Shawn's chest filled with happiness. It was silly looking back, wondering how he could have denied his feelings for Ethan had morphed into something beyond simple friendship.

"So did you want to come with me and the gang up to Mount Baker? We were gonna go Saturday."

Shawn was grateful for the easy conversation, not even hesitating when he agreed to go along.

* * *

As he was attempting to finish getting ready for work, his cell phone started ringing. Grumbling, Shawn hopped on one foot toward the dresser while attempting to put his shoe on. He flipped the phone open without looking at the caller ID and pressed it to his ear. "Greyson." He flopped his foot down and went for his other shoe.

"And here I was thinking it was another pain in the ass I was calling," a feminine voice replied with the hint of laughter.

"Sophia," he greeted, smiling despite himself. "And to what do I owe the pleasure?"

She did laugh then. "Oh bite me, Shawn. Why do you always have to be such a brat?"

"Isn't that what little brothers are for?" he reminded her. She'd said it enough times growing up, after all.

"Agreed."

He grabbed up the rest of his things from the bedroom before heading to the kitchen to find something quick to eat.

"So, I know you're probably trying to get ready for work..."

"But," he supplied with the hint of a grin.

"*But*, I haven't talked to you in ages. You're starting to hurt my feelings."

Shawn chuckled, browsing the fridge. "You know you'll always be my best girl," he assured her.

"Now you're just trying for brownie points."

He grabbed the milk and kicked the door closed behind him, settling on a bowl of cereal. Switching the phone to speaker, he set it on the counter. "Is it working?"

"Maybe a little." He shook his head—still the same old Sophia. "So anyway, that's why I'm calling."

"Because you feel neglected," Shawn clarified.

"Well, that, and 'cause you're going to come hang out with me tonight."

"No can do, Soph. I've got plans." He poured milk over his cereal, plopping in a spoon before putting stuff away.

"Cases can wait."

"Not a case. I have the night off, and I made plans with someone already."

"Oooh, *really*?" The way she dragged the word out, he knew she was about to pry. Sure enough, the first thing Sophia inquired was "Who is she?"

Shawn chuckled. "Not a she."

"Even better!" she chirped. "Do tell."

He laughed at that, deep from his gut. Sophia had always been overenthusiastic when it came to his boyfriends. Perhaps that was to make up for his parents, or maybe it was because she could relate better. Hell, it might have been both. Either way, she was completely incorrigible—not that he'd have it any other way.

"I'm afraid I haven't the time," he teased instead.

"Oh no, Shawn Marcus Greyson! Don't you dare leave me hanging now! Is it anyone I know?"

"No, you haven't met." He had mentioned Ethan to her way back when the accident happened, and Shawn needed someone to talk to about it. Not that he'd brought Ethan up since.

"What's he look like? What's he do? Come on, details!"

He smiled around his spoon, taking the time to chew and swallow before answering. "He's not your type. He's a security consultant. And that's all you need to know."

She huffed. "You're not being very nice, you know. What happened to sharing everything with your dearest sister?"

"You're my only sister," he deadpanned.

"Which is exactly why you should be nice to me. I'm the only one you got," Sophia replied, humor in her voice.

Shawn's smile was fond as he answered honestly, "I know." He paused a moment before offering, "Look, I really do have to get to work. But I promise to call you soon and give you all the juicy details, 'kay?"

"You better," she warned. "I *will* show up there."

"Don't I know it," he answered with a laugh. Sophia was nothing if not tenacious, and it wouldn't be the first time she showed up at his door in a terror, for less.

"Be safe out there, Shawn. I love you."

"Love you too, Soph."

Shawn smiled at the phone as he clicked it off. Having a sister like her was never boring, but he was eternally grateful for it. Still, it would be interesting to see her reaction to Ethan. That was, if anything went anywhere between them.

Tonight would tell the tale.

CHAPTER NINE

Shawn was leaning his shoulder against the wall, brushing a piece of lint he'd missed off his sleeve. He was hoping to appear calm and casual when Ethan came to the door. The man in question looked taken aback when he did so, Shawn grinning brightly in return to hide his nerves.

"All ready?" Shawn asked.

Rather than answer, Ethan commented, "You look really nice." He ducked his head immediately and looked away. "Er, I..." Covering, Ethan plucked at his own button-down and mentioned, "I think I might be underdressed."

Ethan had chosen a nice dress shirt, a plain black with super-thin, vertical white lines, the sleeves rolled up to his elbows. It was tucked into a pair of dark dress denims, with a plain leather belt. Finishing the look was a pair of classic cowboy boots.

Given Shawn's appearance, he couldn't blame Ethan for doubting his choices. Shawn wore a fitted, gray V-neck sweater over a white dress shirt, the collar popped out, and the first button left attractively open. Whereas a pair of jeans wouldn't have looked out of place with it, he instead chose to pair it with black slacks and dress shoes.

Ethan took an unconscious step backward that had Shawn snagging his arm. "Don't be silly," Shawn insisted. His smile was sincere. "You look great."

"Are you sure?" Ethan checked all the same, the hint of a blush on his face.

"Promise. I wouldn't let you feel out of place."

* * *

Ethan's lips quirked up a bit. He knew full well Shawn wasn't the type to be cruel. If he said Ethan was fine, then he was fine. He nudged Shawn out of the way as he stepped from the apartment, locking up.

"And thank you," Shawn mentioned.

"For what?" he asked, tucking his keys into his pocket.

"The compliment earlier."

"Oh, yeah, well..." Ethan shrugged it off, looking away as they made their way down the hall to the elevator. "Right back at you." He felt his mind implode as he mentally screamed. *You are such a dork, Brant. A real freakin' dork.*

When he chanced a glance, he caught Shawn smiling softly to himself and Ethan figured he hadn't screwed up too badly. Then again, what was there to "screw up" exactly? *It's not a date. He just didn't feel like cooking tonight, that's all.* Still, the implication of going *out* together was there in the back of his mind.

* * *

The restaurant was one that Shawn went to sometimes with his sister or—on the rare occasion—a date. It was a waterside establishment out on the islands in the Puget Sound that served fresh catches from the local fishermen. It wasn't unusual for there to be a gathering of people on the beach, surrounding the fire pits and enjoying a few drinks after dinner. Living by the ocean there was no shortage of seafood places, but it was a rare thing to find one that could stand out from the crowd.

"Would you care for the patio?" the hostess inquired. "We have a few open tables out there if you'd prefer not to wait."

Shawn looked to Ethan for an answer. Ethan shrugged and offered, "It's a nice night."

"True enough." Shawn smiled and told her they would take it.

It was pleasant, indeed, out on the patio. As the beginning of autumn was settling in, the temperatures were dropping in the evening. Combined with the breeze coming in off the water, everything was just right for enjoying the outdoor space.

In truth, Shawn was more interested in watching Ethan as he took it all in. Smiling softly, Shawn hid his grin behind the wine list when Ethan looked up.

* * *

"This is a nice place," Ethan mentioned after their drink orders were taken—Shawn having handled the wine selection. "Have you been here before?"

"Quite a few times, actually. Even when it's a full house, it's quiet. And the seafood can't be beat."

It hadn't escaped Ethan's notice how much a mellow atmosphere meant to Shawn. Ethan figured it had a lot to do with being surrounded by noise and chaos all the time at work. It would only make sense that in his downtime Shawn would want to take it as easy as possible.

Speaking of... "Thanks for asking me to come. You didn't have to."

Shawn smiled softly at him, glancing up from the menu. "I look forward to our dinner dates," he replied easily. "Wouldn't want to miss one just because I've been so tired."

Trying to ignore the word *date*, Ethan nodded and pretended to be browsing the menu as he offered, "Well, next time, I'll take you somewhere. My treat."

There was a long pause before Shawn answered quietly, "I would like that." Ethan's eyes darted up to try to catch Shawn's expression, but it was carefully hidden. Even so, it left a warm—if anxious—feeling settling inside him.

When their wine arrived, they placed their orders, and then Shawn held up his glass. "To a successful case and great company." Ethan's lips twisted up as they clinked their glasses together before taking a drink. The sweet flavor of the white wine burst across his palate, and he hummed in approval. "Good?"

Ethan gave a little laugh. "Y'know, I never drank wine before we started hanging out. Think this stuff's growin' on me." He took another sip.

"And just what is your drink of choice then? Wait. Don't tell me...IPA."

Ethan only smiled, causing Shawn to roll his eyes. "Been known to share a shot or two of good bourbon with my ol' man in front of the fire after a hard day."

"Bourbon?"

"Dad's originally from Kentucky. Came out to Montana when he was young, to be a ranch hand. Ended up meeting Ma and the rest is history."

"That...that's actually really sweet."

Ethan's grin was cheeky. "Knew you were a romantic at heart." He nudged Shawn's leg under the table with his foot.

Shawn gave him a meaningful look before changing the topic. Ethan naturally saw through it but let it go. "How'd your appointment with Lynn go?"

"Fine. Missed having you there again." *Oh, that came out wrong,* Ethan mentally chided himself, biting his lip.

"Yeah." Shawn picked at the tablecloth. "Sorry about that."

It hadn't been the first one he missed either, and Ethan got the feeling work was simply an excuse. He looked at Shawn carefully, not saying anything until after their shrimp cocktail arrived. "Don't feel like you have to come on my account." When Shawn just stared off toward the water, Ethan added, "I noticed you weren't really comfortable last time you were there, so..."

* * *

"I'm not good with therapists." Shawn debated about telling Ethan the rest—it wasn't exactly the best dinner conversation—but figured Ethan deserved to know. After all Shawn had been allowed to see of Ethan's troubles, he owed the man that much. "My parents put me in a conversion therapy program when they found out I was bi."

"Shawn—"

"It wasn't one of those camps or anything, and it wasn't for very long, but it still left a sour taste in my mouth over dealing with therapy and, well..." He sighed, managing to meet Ethan's eyes. "Lynn's great; don't get me wrong, but when she tried to press me, all I could think of was that damn doctor sitting there and telling me how *broken* I was and how I was going to Hell."

Ethan reached across the table and rested his hand on top of Shawn's. Neither of them said anything for a bit, simply taking in the mutual comfort. Eventually, Shawn turned his hand around so their palms pressed together, wrapping his fingers around Ethan's hand.

"It was a long time ago," Shawn said quietly, reminding himself in the process. "That last session with Lynn... I was having a bad day 'cause I was thinking about my old partner."

The waitress came over to check on them, and they both silently agreed to start eating their appetizer, though they also never released each other's hands.

"Romantic partner or...?"

"No, Austin was my patrol partner. He was stabbed and..." Shawn sighed. "There was no saving him." He looked at his free hand, almost able to see it covered in bright-red blood from Austin's neck. "He died in my arms, and I was thinking about how I almost lost another one that night with you and—"

Ethan squeezed his hand. "Still here," he reminded him.

Shawn quirked his lips. "Yeah," he murmured fondly, "you are."

Their eyes met, and after a moment, Ethan inquired lightheartedly, "So did you finish that book?"

Shawn barked out a laugh, just threw his head all the way back and laughed deeply from his gut. "Seriously?" He continued to laugh, shaking his head. "You're something else, Brant."

"Happy to be of help." Ethan smiled cheekily.

Shawn grinned in return, more than happy to bring life back into their evening. "Finally finished it," he confirmed. It was the western he was reading the day Ethan had stopped by to meditate. "I'll have to let you borrow it. Turned out to be pretty good."

"Well, I do believe you mentioned gay cowboys." Ethan chuckled, adding with a wink, "I believe that's right up my alley."

They settled into more easy banter about work and family—minus any talk of Shawn's parents—while they ate their shrimp. Neither of them said a word about how their hands hadn't parted until dinner arrived.

* * *

Once the check was settled, Shawn looked out at the water and back to Ethan. "No reason to waste such a beautiful night."

Taking the hint, Ethan smiled softly and suggested, "Let's go for a walk then."

Shawn grinned and offered his hand. Deciding it was too late to turn back, Ethan slid their palms together, allowing Shawn to lead him down to the beach. Shawn looked over at him, offering an endearing little smile. Ethan shook his head, bumping their shoulders together as he chuckled. Shawn only threaded their fingers and pulled him closer.

They had gone far enough to have some privacy, the artificial light of the restaurant and other businesses in the distance. Instead, they were bathed in moonlight, the stars twinkling above them. Ethan tilted his head back, smiling up at the sky. "Miss the stars," he mentioned. "Too hard to see 'em in the city."

Light pollution was a major downside of living in an urban landscape. Ethan missed the open spaces and the wild noises instead of the people and traffic. The only time he had really been in nature since going to college was for weekend retreats or day trips with his friends—whether that was camping in the mountains, fishing out in the Sound, or hiking through the national forests.

"Come on," Ethan encouraged, plopping down in the sand. It was coarser than a typical white sandy beach—more like pebbles that had been smoothed by the water.

Shawn raised his brows, sparing a glance to his dress pants. Sighing, he sat cross-legged beside Ethan. "You owe me dry cleaning," Shawn remarked, attempting a straight face and failing.

Ethan burst out laughing and grabbed Shawn's arm, tugging backward. Shawn let out a yelp and flailed as he went down. "Just shut up and enjoy the view," Ethan chided. Shawn huffed but eventually settled, ignoring Ethan's smirk.

Lying on their backs side by side, they listened to the soft lapping of water. Ethan rolled his head to the right and found that Shawn was looking at him, smiling gently. He couldn't help grinning back, caught up in the look of pure happiness on Shawn's face.

Without thought, Ethan moved his hand up to where Shawn's rested between their shoulders. His fingers threaded with Shawn's, curling around them. It wasn't a handhold, not really, and the simple touch caused a jolt of energy to pass through Ethan, settling into his gut.

Shawn's smile only grew, his fingers brushing back in the lightest of touches. Ethan's chest actually ached, his hand twisting so their palms pressed together. His thumb rubbed against Shawn's, his focus on their joined hands. There was a slight tug that drew his gaze up to Shawn's eyes.

Moonlight brushed against Shawn's fair skin, casting half his face in shadow as Shawn rolled to his left side. Propped up on his elbow, he never released Ethan's hand as he leaned down. Ethan forgot how to breathe when lips brushed against his a moment before their mouths pressed together properly.

* * *

Pulling back enough for their eyes to meet, Shawn looked down into sparkling green orbs. There was no sense in denying his feelings for Ethan any longer, nor did he want to. His free hand brushed across Ethan's cheek, the man coming up to meet him for another kiss.

Ethan grabbed at his shoulder, and Shawn tangled his fingers in Ethan's hair. Shawn tilted his head for a better angle, the passion of their embrace practically overwhelming him. Even so, he never wanted it to end.

Of course, Mother Nature had other ideas. The tide had been coming in as they lay there on the beach, and a wave chose that moment to sweep under their legs. The cool water had them both gasping. Shawn sat up like a shot, Ethan laughing beside him as he did the same.

"Damn that's cold," Ethan griped, causing Shawn to chuckle then as well.

"Yeah." Shawn was smiling, his voice low and teasing as he leaned in. "I can warm you up though." He cut off Ethan's laughter with a gentle kiss.

"You're so cheesy," Ethan teased right back. He made a squeaking sound when another wave came in.

Shawn stood, pulling Ethan up with him. "Guess I should get you home before you end up with a cold."

"Thought you were warming me up?" Ethan reminded him, being the one to steal a kiss that time.

"Whenever you want," Shawn assured him, wrapping an arm around Ethan's waist and steering him back toward the car.

* * *

Having driven his date back home, Shawn made sure to walk him up to his apartment. "Are you always such a gentleman?" Ethan inquired, not bothering to hide the cheekiness in his tone.

"Try to be." Shawn leaned against the doorframe, allowing Ethan to unlock his door.

"So I'm gonna guess that means you'll turn me down if I invite you in?" Ethan let the door swing open pointedly, looking over at Shawn.

"I would have to decline," Shawn agreed. It wasn't his style to just jump into bed with someone, but he did lean in to brush his lips across Ethan's cheek. "I don't think I have to tell you I had a great time tonight."

"Me too." Ethan gave him a smile, hand running down his arm lightly.

"Sleep tight." Shawn pressed his lips to Ethan's one last time. "See you later."

"Tomorrow," Ethan reminded him, speaking of the planned trip into the mountain with his friends.

"Tomorrow," Shawn echoed with a tender smile. "Goodnight."

"'Night," Ethan murmured.

Shawn waited until he heard the dead bolt turn before taking his leave, a huge grin on his face as he stuffed his hands into his pockets.

The night had gone better than he ever could have imagined.

CHAPTER TEN

Everything fell together after that. There wasn't any awkwardness between them the next day; they simply went about life as they had been. The only difference, of course, being that they were doing things as a couple. Well, a *real* couple, since they realized that was what they'd been doing all along.

It had been nearly two weeks with life simply moving as though nothing much had changed. The autumn air was becoming crisper, the nights colder. It was that strange time of year where they were wearing light clothes during the day and snuggling under blankets on the porch come evening, with the furnace kicking on overnight.

Things were different in some regards, except it was all for the better as far as Shawn could see. For one, Ethan appeared to be much more comfortable in his own skin. He finally seemed to settle into a realm of being happy more often than not.

Shawn, well, he found himself actually taking time off work—something Davies had not shut up about for three days straight. He promised Ethan that the weekends would all be for them. On top of that, Ethan had been able to get Shawn to leave work at a decent hour most of the time. Granted, it was easier the days Ethan was at the station.

"Where's your boy?" Davies inquired, noting the empty chair this morning. There had been talk, with Ethan's success of toning down the amount of time he spent at the station—especially given he and Shawn's new relationship status—though Davies knew nothing had been officially decided yet.

"He's down in the patrol room."

There was no helping the pride on Shawn's face. It had been Ethan's suggestion almost two months previously at therapy, shot down by both Lynn and Shawn at the time. Now, however, Shawn was confident that Ethan would be fine, not even insisting on going with him. Granted, he didn't know what Lynn had to say on the matter since Shawn had yet to return after the scare with her insightfulness.

"Really?" Davies gave a thoughtful hum, looking off toward the door as though Ethan would materialize at any moment. Slapping a file on the desk, he commented, "Hope he steals us some donuts."

It turned out that Ethan did, in fact, swipe a couple of donuts for them, and Shawn could only smile and press a kiss to his cheek in thanks. "Everything go alright?"

"Yeah, it was actually really nice."

"Good." Shawn brushed his hand along Ethan's wrist. "I'll grab you some coffee."

* * *

With Shawn out of sight, Davies stepped next to Ethan and spoke around his bite of donut. "You two are sickeningly sweet." Ethan bumped their shoulders together, smiling up at him around his own donut. "Just make sure you take care of him," Davies added, a bit more seriously. "Lord knows, he has no idea how to do it himself."

Shawn returned, overhearing the last part and scowling at his friend. Ethan laughed while Davies grinned at them both, feigning innocence.

* * *

Shawn was leaning against the kitchen island, sipping at the sweet white wine he'd picked for the evening. Jazz was wafting through the sound system that piped music through the kitchen and living room—even out on the porch if he desired it, which was rare. The baked chicken dish had just been put in the oven, and he was taking a break before starting on the sides.

He knew the moment Ethan arrived, and not just because of the soft click of the door. Rather, it was the music change not a minute later as Ethan hijacked the stereo system via the Bluetooth on his smartphone. Shawn just shook his head as the soft melody of some country tune drifted from the speakers.

When Ethan walked in there was no helping the smile on Shawn's face, even though he was still shaking his head in amusement. "I was listening to something," he pointed out.

"This is better," Ethan assured him, leaning in to kiss him softly in greeting. Shawn knew it was pointless to argue.

One day, Shawn would have to figure out how to turn off the Bluetooth function so that Ethan would no longer be able to do that. It had only taken until the second or third visit for Ethan to find it completely by accident. He had been looking at his playlist for a song he'd wanted Shawn to hear, grinning as he sent it to the stereo, and it had played out of the speakers all around them.

"That's debatable." Shawn set his glass aside, pulling Ethan into his arms and giving him another, deeper kiss. "Just for that, you get to chop the onions." Ethan made a face, but he smiled when Shawn swatted his hip.

Later, while they were enjoying what was to be a quiet evening leading into an equally quiet weekend, Shawn's cell phone went off. "Greyson," Captain Sanchez said on the other end, "we have a situation."

When Shawn hung up the phone, he sighed. "Home invasion," he explained without prompting. "One dead, another in critical condition."

Ethan frowned. "Guess that means you need to go in?"

"Sorry, babe," Shawn apologized immediately.

"It's okay," Ethan reassured him. "Don't worry about it. They need you. I get it." It wasn't until he gave Shawn an encouraging half smile that Shawn relented.

"Alright, I shouldn't be long."

Shawn went into the bedroom and slipped on his shoulder holster. He grabbed his Glock from the small safe in the closet, checking it out of habit. Releasing the magazine to make sure it was loaded, he then pulled the slide back a bit, confirming a round was chambered. Satisfied, he popped the magazine back in before sliding it home in its holster.

He returned to the living room to find Ethan had already grabbed his trench coat from the closet. Ethan passed it over, returning Shawn's smile. After putting on his coat, Shawn accepted his keys as well, taking the one for the house off the ring.

"Here," he offered to Ethan. "Like I said, I shouldn't be long, but if it gets too late, and you wanna go, I understand. I have a spare hidden outside, so just lock up behind you." He pressed a kiss to the corner of Ethan's mouth. "Feel free to stay as long as you like though," he quickly added.

"I'll be fine," Ethan assured him, stealing a proper kiss before urging him out the door. "Be safe," he called after him.

"Always." Shawn held up his hand in farewell and then popped the collar of his coat up against the cool breeze of the night.

Hopefully he wouldn't be long. All Shawn could already think of was coming back to Ethan.

* * *

When he arrived home, the house was dark. Shawn had figured his boyfriend would end up leaving and was grateful the porch light had been left on for him. He reached up to the back of one of the pillars that framed the front stoop and opened the small hidden compartment containing the spare key.

Inside, he hung his coat in the closet and then made his way into the kitchen to grab something to drink. He snagged a bottle of water, the soft glow of the undercabinet lighting enough to see by. It also allowed him to spot the key on the counter.

Curious, Shawn made his way through the house to the bedroom, finding Ethan fast asleep. A smile crossed his face, warmth spreading through him at the sight of Ethan in his bed. It wasn't what he expected to return to, but he was more than happy nonetheless.

He dressed for bed quietly, not wanting to disturb Ethan. However, as soon as Shawn slipped under the covers, he stirred. Blinking at him sleepily, it took a moment before Ethan gave him a lopsided smile. "Hey," Ethan greeted. "You're back."

"I am." Shawn smiled softly back, leaning down to give Ethan a kiss. "Go back to sleep."

Ethan reached up and grabbed Shawn, pulling him down into his arms. It was the first time they'd spent the night together, and for Shawn, it felt like coming home. "I love you," Shawn murmured, lips brushing against a cheekbone as he voiced aloud what he'd known for some time.

He could hear the grin in Ethan's voice. "Love you too."

Shawn's arms curled around him, tugging as he rolled to his back. Ethan looked down at him, chuckling. He adjusted so most of his weight rested on his knees and legs rather than on Shawn. "I *was* sleeping, you know," Ethan reminded him, smiling all the same.

"Good dreams?" Shawn asked, hands on Ethan's hips. His fingers went under the borrowed shirt Ethan wore, drifting lightly across skin and causing a shiver to run up Ethan's spine.

"Thinking this is better," Ethan breathed out softly. He gazed at Shawn, only illuminated by the streetlight that snaked through the blinds. Ethan was looking at him like he was the world, and it melted Shawn's heart.

Ethan sat up and raised his arms when Shawn tugged at his shirt, allowing him to pull it off and toss it aside. His hands ran down Ethan's chest and over his abdomen, brushing over the scar there, before settling back on his hips. There was a twist to Shawn's lips as his fingers trailed beneath the elastic of Ethan's pajama pants.

"Sit up," Ethan ordered, yanking Shawn's shirt off to join the other on the floor. He didn't hesitate to pull Shawn into a kiss. It was anything but tame, filled with intent as Ethan's fingers dug into Shawn's sides, and their tongues curled together. Shawn pulled Ethan with him as he lay back down, pressing together along their lengths while they let hands wander on newly exposed flesh.

When Ethan finally moved away for air, he sat up, shifting to settle more fully on Shawn's hips. The quicker rise and fall of Shawn's chest must have pulled Ethan's gaze to the tattoo along his left ribcage. Ethan's fingers traced the scripted letters. Of course his fingers ended up wandering then, drifting down Shawn's lightly toned core before hooking into his waistband.

Sex wasn't something they'd pushed for, each more than content to let it happen in its own time. Ethan smirked down at Shawn, meeting his eyes. "So, you weren't like a Boy Scout or anything, were you?"

Shawn barked out a laugh, shaking his head. "No. But I assure you I'm very prepared for just this situation." Ethan's smile grew, and Shawn couldn't help reaching up to cup his cheek. "Come here, you," he murmured, latching his fingers around Ethan's neck and pulling him down for another soft kiss.

* * *

Out of nowhere, Ethan went silent.

Shawn called his cell in the morning while making tea, wanting to let him know to dress for the weather. He was going to surprise Ethan by taking him along to a scene he wanted a second look at. Perhaps they could even brainstorm together on a few things. Except there was no answer.

Brushing it off, Shawn drove over to the apartment. After all, Ethan could have been in the shower or just getting ready.

When he knocked on Ethan's door, there was no response. Brows dropping, he grabbed his cell and tried another call. Once again, he received the voice mail. Shawn pressed redial, his ear to the door to see if he could hear the answering ring—or really anything—but no such luck. When further knocking produced no results, he decided to leave a voice mail.

"Hey, babe, are you okay? I'm outside your place, and it doesn't look like you're home." With as much racket as he made, if Ethan had simply slept in, he would have been awakened. "Did you get called into work or something? Call me."

Hanging up, he noted one of Ethan's neighbors coming out of his own apartment. The older man huffed when he saw Shawn, turning to lock his door. "He left earlier," he informed Shawn. "'Bout knocked me down in the stairwell."

Shawn was reminded of what Ethan had told him, how living in an apartment meant knowing everyone's business. "Did you catch where he was going?"

"Nope. Apologized, but he was in a hurry. Distracted by somethin'." The man paused at the stairwell entrance. "Hope he's alright. Good kid. My wife worried about him after that accident of his. She always liked having a cop livin' down the hall."

"Thanks," Shawn replied with a polite nod, moving to call the elevator.

It felt strange for him to head into work alone.

* * *

"Any messages for me?" Shawn greeted Davies.

"No?" was the confused response.

"I don't get it." At Davies's raised brow, he explained, "Ethan wasn't home when I went to pick him up, and he's not answering the phone."

"That's weird," Davies agreed with a frown. "Family emergency?"

"I would think he'd have called." He dropped his satchel on the desk with a *thud*. "Maybe something came up at work." Shawn didn't sound very convinced himself.

"Well, wait a bit, and if he still doesn't pick up, call his office."

Shawn nodded, attempting to focus on his work. Not that he was successful. He couldn't concentrate with all the possibilities rolling around in his head.

He picked up the landline at his desk, ignoring Davies's pointed look, and called Ethan's cell once more. When he got voice mail again, Shawn didn't bother to hide his concern. "Hey, it's me. What's going on? Is something wrong? You're making me worried here, babe. Call me, please."

It didn't last more than thirty seconds before Shawn was looking up the number to the security firm Ethan worked for. When the receptionist picked up, he asked to speak to Ethan and was put on hold. "I'm sorry, sir," the woman spoke when she returned to the line. "It appears Mr. Brant isn't in today."

"Is he out with a client?" Shawn inquired, knowing she probably wasn't allowed to divulge the information yet trying anyway.

"I'm sorry, but I don't know. Did you want to leave him a message?"

"No, no message. Thanks."

When he set the phone in its cradle, he noticed Davies watching him. "No luck?" Shawn shook his head. "I don't like this." At least Shawn wasn't the only one concerned now. "When was the last time you talked to him?"

"Yesterday at lunch." Ethan had been at the office, not feeling up to going out to meet for a quick meal. "I tried calling him after work, but he didn't pick up. Got a text right after that saying he was still at work and busy, so I told him to call me later. He never did. And then, when I finally noticed the time, it was late. Called anyway but wasn't really concerned when he didn't answer." Shawn figured Ethan had gotten home late and crashed in bed out of exhaustion.

Davies continued to frown. "Dunno, Greyson. Something stinks."

"He might just be out at a site," Shawn reasoned, more to settle his own nerves than anything. "Could have been something last minute, and he's tied up."

Davies didn't seem convinced but let it go while Shawn attempted to distract himself with work.

* * *

Lunchtime rolled around with no word from Ethan. "Call the hospitals," Davies said, standing beside Shawn's desk. Clearly, he was worried as well. "I'll try calling him and see if he'll pick up for me."

Shawn didn't want to admit that his mind had wandered down a similar path. Ethan could have had a panic attack, unable to stop. It wasn't as though his PTSD were simply *gone*, no matter how well he was doing as of late. The idea that Ethan might be hurt made him feel sick.

Focus.

"Yes, this is Detective Greyson. Is there an Ethan Brant admitted? How about any John Does admitted in the last twenty-four hours?"

When he hung up he noticed Davies was speaking on the phone and perked up. "Alright," Davies was saying, "just get ahold of him soon, okay? You made us worry."

"Ethan?" Shawn asked hopefully when Davies set his phone aside.

"Yeah, got voice mail and then a text. Said he was fine but I told 'im a text wasn't gonna cut it, and he better pick up the phone." *Smart.* It could have been anyone using Ethan's phone.

"So he's okay? Where is he?"

"Wouldn't say. Just said he was fine. Wasn't in any kind of trouble. He's apparently busy with something and just needs some space."

Shawn frowned. *What the hell is that supposed to mean?*

"Not sure what's going on," Davies continued, "but at least we know he's not lying in a gutter somewhere." Davies wasn't happy about Ethan's behavior either; that was clear.

"Yeah," Shawn answered softly. "Guess so."

He didn't get much work done that day.

CHAPTER ELEVEN

By the next afternoon Shawn had had enough of the radio silence. He was far past worried and had moved into anger. If there was nothing wrong with Ethan, then that meant there was something wrong with *them*. And if that was the case, then Shawn figured he was at least owed some kind of explanation.

Once again, Ethan wasn't answering his door when Shawn stopped by after work. Huffing, he pulled out his lock-picking tools and settled on one knee as he got to work.

If he'd picked up one skill while at the department, it was getting into places no one wanted him to be and doing it quietly. Therefore the simple doorknob lock was nothing. He was only mildly disappointed the dead bolt and chain weren't on the door, but it got him in, so he wasn't about to complain.

Shawn wasn't sure if Ethan was even home. He moved quietly, walking into the living room where the TV was on. Except there was no one to be found.

"Shawn?" He spun to find Ethan coming down the short hall from the bedroom. "What are you doing here?"

"Why haven't you answered your phone?" Shawn demanded in turn. "Why haven't you *called*?"

Ethan stopped out of reach, an incredulous look on his face. "Seriously? So you literally just *broke into my place* 'cause I haven't returned your calls?"

Well, when you say it like THAT... Shawn's moment of sheepishness didn't last. It wasn't his fault Ethan had gone dark like that and made Shawn worried sick. "You could have at least let me know you were alright!" he snapped.

They were interrupted when another man stepped from the bathroom, nothing but a towel around his waist. He was tall and lean, with dark skin and features that suggested Native American roots— though not likely full-blooded, given his eyes appeared more honey-colored than brown.

Rubbing at his shoulder-length hair with another towel, the man paused to take in the scene before him.

Shawn's shock quickly turned to anger. "Oh, well, I see." He scowled at Ethan, not even able to believe he was the kind of person that would pull something like this. "You could have just *told* me."

As he headed for the door, Ethan followed. "Wait! It's not what it looks like." He grabbed Shawn's arm, spinning him around and pushing his back against the door. "I'm sorry I didn't call you. That was wrong of me, I know. It's just..." Ethan sighed, eyes looking down. "I had some...things to work out."

The stranger was leaning against the corner, watching them closely. Ethan glanced over his shoulder and back up at Shawn. "This is my best friend, Sebastian Giroux." Well that name confirmed his initial assessment. "And this is my idiot of a boyfriend."

"Says the guy who doesn't return phone calls" was Shawn's petulant reply.

"Says the guy who just committed a B & E."

Sebastian chuckled. "You two are adorable."

Ethan huffed, telling him, "Go put on some damn clothes!" Rolling his eyes dramatically, Sebastian disappeared toward the bedroom. With a defeated sigh, Ethan grabbed Shawn's hand. "I think we need to talk," he said unnecessarily, leading Shawn over to the couch and encouraging him to sit.

Shawn felt his stomach drop out from under him.

* * *

"What the hell is going on, Ethan?" Shawn no longer seemed angry, just upset. Ethan couldn't exactly blame him.

"I'm sorry for being such an ass. I know I should have let you know I was alright, I just..." He closed his eyes tightly a moment. "I needed some space to think."

"About what?" Shawn shifted nervously, obviously expecting the worst.

"I sent myself into a panic. About us."

Shawn's confused expression was understandable.

"Everything between us just happened so fast," Ethan explained. "And I—I got scared that we were in so deep so quickly."

"But...everything's been great between us," Shawn ventured. "Or at least, I thought it was."

"It has been," Ethan assured him, his lips twitching up at the corner. "I got frightened, though, that it was all going to just crash and burn at any minute and—"

Shawn cut him off with a kiss. Ethan melted into it, feeling nothing but love for Shawn in this moment. "Stop overthinking," Shawn chastised, a smile against Ethan's lips. "I love you. That's all you need to know."

"I love you too." It was Ethan who kissed him that time before giving them some space so he could look at Shawn properly. "I've never had a relationship just...*work* like this. And I freaked out, and I was stupid, and..." Ethan groaned, leaning sideways into the cushions, head lying on the back of the couch. "I'm sorry. I didn't mean to make you worry like that. I just needed to clear my head."

"And get your ass kicked." Sebastian joined them in a painted-on pair of jeans and fitted shirt with a pride flag on it. Sitting on the loveseat that partially faced them, he held out his hand to Shawn. "Call me Bastian by the way." Shawn nodded as he accepted Sebastian's hand. "When he decided to start having an existential crisis, I drove up here."

"And I regret it," Ethan snarked, getting a little of his old fire back, which made Shawn smirk.

"I set him straight though, I think," Sebastian assured him, looking at Shawn. "He's a complete moron sometimes, but he really does love you, and that says something."

Ethan wasn't looking at either of them as he defended, "It's not like I've had a lot of relationships to go off of here, okay?"

Growing up in a small town, being gay wasn't exactly easy. Even if he'd known anyone else who swung that way, Ethan doubted they would have really been able to date. As a kid he would have been too scared of the consequences, even when his parents supported who he was.

"Never dated until college," Ethan continued. "You think most guys that age are more interested in steady partners or just sex?"

Reaching over, Shawn brushed his fingers across the back of Ethan's hand. "I promise that's not what I want. Just sex, I mean."

"I know. Pretty sure I figured that out after it took me two weeks to finally get in your pants." Ethan chuckled as he laced their fingers together. He sobered a little as he added, "Told you it was all stupid."

"Well, next time you decide to be stupid, how about at least giving me a heads-up." Shawn had the hint of a teasing grin on his face when Ethan looked at him.

"Sounds like a plan." After a moment, Ethan smirked. "Guess this means I should probably get you your own key."

Ethan ended up with his ass on the floor after receiving a shove from Shawn.

* * *

Having gone out for proper groceries, Shawn was directing the activity in the small kitchen. It appeared Sebastian had a far better concept of cooking than Ethan did—which was appreciated—and he jumped right in without complaint.

"Don't cut yourself, Buttercup," Sebastian teased Ethan as he was chopping up an onion.

"Bite me, Cupcake."

Shawn snickered, feigning innocence when Ethan cut him a look. Deciding not to comment, Shawn asked Sebastian, "So where are you from?"

"The Flathead Reservation," he answered. "Ironically enough, it's not far from where this one grew up," he indicated Ethan.

"I'm not familiar with it," Shawn replied apologetically.

Sebastian shrugged it off. "'S alright. Our confederation is made of a few tribes, but I'm Kootenai."

"I honestly don't know much about different tribes," Shawn admitted. "You'll have to tell me about them sometime."

"Sure." Sebastian didn't seem bothered by Shawn's ignorance at all. Flipping his hair—which had curled after drying—from his face, he looked at Shawn. "It's honestly not that unusual. I've become somewhat of a resource for the bureau on the subject."

Shawn had known one of Ethan's friends from Seattle University was in the FBI, so he wasn't all that surprised to learn it was Sebastian. "How'd you convince this one to go into law enforcement?" he asked instead, with a little smirk.

It was Ethan who answered, "By being persistent."

"He was all set for his business degree," Sebastian explained.

"Which I still ended up getting," Ethan reminded him.

Even after joining the force, Ethan had been determined to see his degree through. The whole point of him getting it was so that he could aid the ranch. He may not have been as involved as originally planned, but he was still helping where he could while being hundreds of miles away.

Sebastian continued as though uninterrupted, "But since he was helping me so much with my own stuff, I ended up convincing him to go into law enforcement."

"Why not the FBI?" Shawn asked, looking between them both.

"I wanted to be able to go back home," Ethan explained. "But they hired me here right away. And there was nothing near Silver Creek at the time, so I took it as a way to get my foot in the door."

Shawn nodded. "Not a bad tactic." He hesitated before asking what was sure to be a delicate question. "Thinkin' maybe you'll still do it? Go back home and do something there?"

Ethan gave a halfhearted shrug. It was Sebastian who answered, "Told 'em the Sheriff's K-9 Unit was still an option."

"K-9 Unit?"

"He never told you?" When Shawn shook his head, Sebastian said, "Yeah, that was the goal."

"I love dogs," Ethan interjected. "Thought it was a natural choice."

"We were never allowed pets, growing up," Shawn commented, attempting to turn the conversation away from the shaky topic.

Ethan appeared relieved. "We've always had dogs. Blue heelers mostly. At least one or two at a time. They're a big help on the ranch, but they're more than that to us.

"Haven't had one in a while though," he continued. "Sage had to get put down last year. Just got too old. Colt…" Ethan sighed. "Last fall he got kicked in the head moving the herd. Died instantly."

"Sorry to hear that," Shawn murmured.

"Thanks. He was a special one. I think that's why they haven't looked for another one. That an' I've gotta sneakin' suspicion that my folks are waitin' on me to come home. Pick a pup out together. Willing to bet that'll change soon though," Ethan said with a smile. "Rumor has it Colt's sister is gonna be havin' a litter. Ma won't be able to resist."

Shawn only smiled slightly in return. He didn't really know what having a pet was like. The idea of getting one with Ethan, though, was tempting. The thought made his smile grow.

After asking Ethan to mince some garlic next, Shawn turned his focus to the stove. He started the water to steam the vegetables Sebastian had prepped while Shawn was working on the meat.

"FBI seems an odd choice for someone growing up on a reservation," Shawn mentioned. "I mean, it's not as though the tribes and federal authorities have the best history."

"Oh, I'm all kinds of popular back on the rez." Sebastian laughed. "I think most of 'em figure it's the *white man* in me."

Ethan gave him a suggestive grin. "You mean the white *blood* in you, or the white guy that was bangin' ya at the time?"

Shawn burst out laughing, head thrown back, the others laughing right along. "Oh my God, you are awful!" he told his boyfriend.

"Did I lie?" Ethan challenged his best friend in turn.

"I'm pretty sure I was banging *him*, but other than that..." Sebastian couldn't get through his comment without more laughing.

Shawn shoved Sebastian's shoulder. "I stand corrected. You're both awful."

"I will not apologize for my healthy sex life."

Shawn shook his head, chuckling. Although after a couple of minutes of companionable silence while getting everything on the stove, he couldn't help but ask, "So they're not happy about you being gay, I take it?"

Sebastian shrugged. "It's a mixed bag. But then, that just comes with the territory. Back before our culture was subverted, no one cared. With Christianity, came their feelings on same-sex relationships though, and that caused a rift."

"But your parents?"

"Them? No, they don't care at all."

Shawn hummed thoughtfully. "Wish I knew what that was like."

Ethan tilted his head, looking as though he wanted to ask. Instead, he let it go for all of a minute. "My dad was *freaked* when I came out." He had Shawn's attention then. "I told Matty first. Testing the waters, y'know? 'Course he didn't care at all and told me I should tell our folks. Yeah..."

"So your dad doesn't approve?" Shawn ventured gently, not wanting to step on any sore spots—he'd done enough of that already that night.

"Oh, he came around. Mom just hugged me and told me she loved me. Dad...Dad was really quiet, and then he got up and left the house. I honestly thought I was gonna get kicked out, but he didn't do a damn thing. He just... He never acknowledged it. Then, out of the blue, he just looked at me and told me it was alright."

"Just like that?" Ethan nodded, and Shawn looked away to hide how dejected he felt.

It was Sebastian who asked Shawn, "I take it your coming-out didn't go so well?"

"You can say that."

"You don't have to talk about it," Ethan offered quietly.

Shawn shrugged, leaning against the counter. "My father refused to speak to me *at all*. There was no just ignoring the topic. It was radio silence, period." He gave a short, bitter laugh. "And my *mother*... That was a trip and a half. Hauling me off to church, throwing girls at me. Awful does not begin to describe it."

Ethan and Sebastian winced in sympathy. Shawn tried not to dwell on it. He wasn't the first person with a shitty family.

"When I see them now," Shawn continued, "I'm lucky if my father says all of two words to me. And my mother's sure to ask if I'm dating a nice girl. She pretty much just lives in her own state of denial." Another humorless laugh left his mouth. "Hell, that's my whole family though. We ignore my father's affairs, my mother's drinking, and the fact I like to take men as well as women to bed." He gave an unkind smile. "Good times."

Ethan pressed against Shawn's side, nose going to the crook of his neck as he offered silent support.

"Got us now," Sebastian told him, metaphorically extending his own hand as well.

Shawn gave Sebastian a grateful half smile, arm wrapping around Ethan and dropping a kiss on the top of his head. That part of his life was over. It was time to look ahead.

CHAPTER TWELVE

"You are a menace," Ethan concluded, his little brother's laughter filling the room as it exited the speakers on the laptop.

"That's what they keep telling me." Matt stuck his tongue out, scrunching his nose cheekily. "So now that you've heard my woeful tale of the week, it's your turn. What's the latest gossip?"

"What is this? A sewing circle?"

"Oh shit. I forgot my knitting. Hold on!"

Ethan rolled his eyes, laughing heartily. "Nothing much" was his reply once he'd managed to calm himself a bit. "Keeping busy with work."

"*And*?" Matt prodded, waving his hand in a circle.

"Why's there have to be an 'and'?"

"Oh there is *definitely* an 'and.' I'd know that avoidance maneuver anywhere."

"I'd throw a pillow at you," Ethan stated, "but all that would accomplish would be hurting my computer."

"Gotcha covered, bro," Matt replied, snatching up the pillow on his bed and whacking himself in the face. Ethan clutched his sides from laughing, bending over until his forehead rested on a knee. "So, *spill*. Tell me all your dirty little secrets!"

Ethan was too busy trying to catch his breath, barely hearing the apartment door open. He was still shaking with laughter as he turned to look over his shoulder. From his place on the couch, he could see Shawn set a bag of groceries on the counter. "Hey," Ethan managed to croak out in greeting before breaking down into another fit of laughter.

* * *

"What in the world are you on?" Shawn questioned with a raised brow. He stopped off to hang his trench coat by the door before coming farther into the room. As he sat next to his boyfriend, he saw Skype open with a younger version of Ethan staring back at him.

A lighter brown, the kid's hair was kept at a manageable length though obviously *un*managed. There was a little scruffy facial hair to match the unkempt image. His hazel eyes gazed at Shawn curiously before returning to Ethan and back again. Ethan's photos may have been a bit out of date, but there was no denying this was Matt.

Ethan smiled over at Shawn, gesturing to the screen. "Meet my baby bro, Matty."

"Hey!" the teen protested. Ethan laughed at his expense and Matt snorted. "When'd you get a roomie, dude?"

When Ethan ducked his head, Shawn smirked over at him. "Oh this should be good." Shawn threw his arm onto the back of the couch, foot coming up to rest on the opposite knee.

Ethan muttered a "Fuck off" under his breath before looking at Matt. "Why must you notice everything?" he complained. Apparently it hadn't escaped Matt that Shawn had let himself in. "This is Shawn. My new boyfriend."

"Boyfriend!" Matt moved closer to the camera then. "Why the fuck didn't you tell me?"

"Umm, well..."

"This totally isn't a new thing!" Matt barreled on. "I mean the dude has a *key*. Why do you do these things to me? Seriously, bro, not cool."

"Are ya done, drama queen?" Ethan asked plainly, though there was no missing the amusement on his face.

Matt sniffed, leaning back and crossing his arms over his chest. "For now."

"To answer your question there, butthead, I wanted to tell Mom and Dad first."

"They don't know either? E!"

"Well, I wanted to be sure things were serious first," he argued.

"Ahem, the man has a *key*. I think we've gotten to the point of serious."

Shawn had pulled his hand up to cover his mouth, trying so hard not to laugh at the Brant boys. His snicker drew Ethan's attention, and Shawn threw his hands up in surrender. "Don't look at me. The kid has a point."

"See!"

"And wasn't that the whole reason I ended up with a key anyway?" Shawn mused, referring to his lock-picking. "'Cause it was getting too serious, too fast?"

"You can both go suck it," Ethan answered.

"Oh, don't pout," Shawn replied with a fond smile, leaning forward to kiss the wrinkles between Ethan's brows. "You know I'm teasing." Shawn knew he'd get hit for it, but he couldn't help adding, "Though you're cute when you pout."

Sure enough, he received a smack to the gut. It was completely worth it as Ethan was smiling. "Brat," Ethan muttered, even as he was leaning in to give Shawn a soft kiss on the lips. "Love you."

"Love you too," he murmured, stealing another kiss.

"Aren't y'all so cute." Matt's voice broke them apart, and they looked at the screen to find him making a kissy face, complete with noises.

"I told ya he was a little shit," Ethan mentioned, Shawn only chuckling in reply.

Matt didn't help his case when he set the laptop down in front of himself and then rolled on the bed to lie on his stomach. Chin in hands, he kicked his feet, a playful smile on his face. "Sooo, how'd you two meet?" he asked, his voice pitched in a mockery of feminine gossip.

"See what I mean?" Ethan gruffed.

Matt laughed, dropping the act and saying, "Seriously though..."

* * *

Ethan licked his lips, insides doing a little flip-flop. He didn't like to talk about the accident with his brother. Part of that had to do with the fact Ethan had neglected to tell Matt about his PTSD or therapy; Matt didn't need to worry about him. Matt looked up to him, and Ethan didn't want to ruin the image of the big brother and protector.

"Shawn's the one who saved my life that night."

Matt's brows rose. "Yeah?" He looked to Shawn as he said, "Dude... I can't even begin to thank you."

"Don't mention it," Shawn replied.

Ethan knew better than anyone that Shawn hadn't done it for the thanks or praise. Looking over at him, Shawn gave a little, encouraging smile before pressing a kiss to Ethan's forehead.

"Don't worry, Matt," Shawn assured him, arm wrapping around Ethan's shoulders as he looked back at the computer. "Promise, I'm taking care of him."

Ethan nudged him but was grinning all the same. "No complaints here."

* * *

"Sophia," Ethan greeted, pressing a kiss to the woman's cheek. Shawn did the same to her other cheek, and Sophia smiled at them as they sat.

The slinky black dress Sophia wore clung to her curves, showing off long legs. Her necklace, dazzling with sapphires, brought out the blue in her eyes. They matched Shawn's to a T, as did her long, wavy strawberry-blonde hair, which she tossed casually over her shoulder.

It wasn't their first dinner together. Ethan could recall their initial meeting. Sophia had taken a long gander at him before turning to Shawn and stating plainly, "You're not supposed to have hotter boyfriends than me." When it had been pointed out that she had no boyfriend to speak of, her response had been, "I know. But this one's going to be hard to top." Naturally, Ethan had been blushing the entire time.

They had started to make it a fairly regular occasion to meet for brunch or dinner on the weekends since then. It was, however, their first time in a place as fancy as Chateau Ste. Michelle Winery. Shawn even had to take Ethan out for new dress pants and then spoiled him by adding in a blue, silk dress shirt as well.

"Just getting you used to the poshness," Sophia supplied as Ethan took in their surroundings.

"Dunno," Ethan mused. "Shawn's never wanted to go to a place like this before."

Shawn smirked at his sister. "That's his way of saying I'm not a snob like you."

Sophia laughed, a melodic sound that carried through the space without being intrusive. Ethan was certain it was a learned skill. He'd heard plenty of stories from both Greysons on their ability to blend in with the high-society crowd their parents surrounded themselves with. Not that either of them were fake—not with Ethan at least—though he saw how easily they could chameleon themselves if the need arose.

"Actually," Ethan supplied, his lips twisted at the corners in amusement, "just confused on why I would *need to get used to it*."

"The holidays are coming up," Sophia offered by way of explanation. Of course, that meant nothing to Ethan, but Shawn groaned.

"No," Shawn told her flatly.

* * *

The waiter came over to inquire about their drink orders, and naturally, Shawn was the one to pick out their wine, Sophia holding up her glass for a refill of her own. She also took the liberty of ordering an appetizer for the table.

Shawn tried to busy himself by looking at the menu, but Sophia wasn't giving in. "Mom and Dad will be expecting you, you know."

"And they can keep right on expecting. Just like they can keep expecting I'll show up and suddenly be *straight* and back in law school."

Shawn knew she had half a mind to blurt out that he wasn't being fair. In a way, that was true. He also didn't care. Their parents hadn't exactly been *fair* to him and certainly never anything resembling loving. They may have provided for him financially, but that was where their support ended.

"They're still your parents," Sophia pointed out. "And it's still the holidays."

"As though that's ever meant anything in our family. All the holidays are to them is a chance to rub elbows and try to impress all their 'friends.' So whatever you're thinking—"

"That I'm not about to go through *another* holiday season listening to them complain about how you didn't show up. Again."

Shawn snorted.

"Please? You can even bring Ethan."

His sister's soft, insistent gaze did nothing to compel him. "Like I wanna expose him to any of those people. Let alone our parents." He huffed out a little humorless laugh. "Besides...I'm sure they'd have something to say about my date of choice."

"Their own fault for leaving the 'plus one' open-ended." She gave him an amused smirk.

"You're horrible," Shawn concluded, redoubling his efforts to ignore her by picking out what he wanted to eat. Not that it worked when he could feel Ethan's eyes on him. "If you've got something to add..." he offered up to no one in particular, although apparently, Ethan got that it was meant for him.

"I'll go with you if it would make things easier."

"You don't know what you're getting yourself into."

"No, you really don't," Sophia agreed. "But I'd appreciate more backup." She offered Ethan a little smile, and Shawn felt a stab of guilt. Sophia had been going to all the family holiday parties, even when

Shawn rarely had attended before he stopped going altogether. He had left her high and dry, something she would never have done to him.

Sighing, Shawn said, "There's no way I'm going to Thanksgiving dinner." It was too personal, stuck at a table with just the family. If he didn't shoot someone, he was liable to pull the trigger on himself instead.

Latching onto the opening he left, Sophia asked, "So you'll come for Christmas then?"

He couldn't believe he was considering this. "The party I guess, yeah, but don't expect me there on the day."

"Oh?" She raised a teasing brow. "Did you have something better to do?"

"I'll probably just sleep in and then drag myself down to the station because 'bah humbug.'"

* * *

Sophia laughed loud and open, the way Shawn did when he was truly happy, and Ethan felt himself relax. The tension eased, Sophia shoving Shawn's shoulder playfully and scolding him for working too much. *Understatement,* Ethan thought.

Of course all the talk about the holidays made him realize he and Shawn had never discussed any plans before then. "I always go home for Christmas and New Year's," Ethan informed him.

"That must be nice," Sophia replied. Ethan had told Sophia all about the ranch and his family the first time they'd arranged for drinks together.

With their meals ordered—somehow they'd managed to look at the menu between Sophia's pressuring—she asked Ethan, "So you go for Thanksgiving too?"

"I did while I was in school, but now I just save the vacation days."

Shawn frowned. "Not even going this year?" Ethan knew Shawn most likely thought it best to be with his family after everything that had happened. Ethan couldn't say that he disagreed, but really, they would all be fine.

"I figured we would spend it together," Ethan answered instead, managing a soft smile. He looked away almost shyly as he admitted, "I was kind of hoping you'd wanna come to the ranch with me when I went.

I know Ma would love for you to come. And Matty's been talkin' 'bout gettin' to meet you in person."

"I, uh, well…" Shawn looked stunned, quickly catching himself. "Sure, I guess. I mean, if you want me to and your parents don't mind."

"Doubt it'd be a problem. I'm sure they'd love to meet you."

Sophia snarked, "You mean you'd actually use some damn vacation days? Mark the calendar!"

"Oh, bite me."

She stuck her tongue out at Shawn.

"Petulant brat," he remarked.

"Uptight priss," she countered.

Ethan laughed, shaking his head. They were siblings through and through. There was no missing the deep, loving bond they shared though. It reminded him so much of Matt, and it made him miss his little brother even more.

"If you're going to your folks' place though…" Ethan began.

Sophia was the one to answer. "Oh, they host like a week before. It's the posh thing to do, don't you know." Shawn grunted. "Scrooge here will be sure to keep you informed."

"Christmas is a spectacle," Shawn argued. "It's hardly what I'd call a *joyous occasion*. Everything's so commercialized, it's pathetic."

"I started seeing Christmas stuff out *before* Halloween," Ethan lamented. Shawn had worried Ethan was a holiday freak when he went all out on Halloween—wearing vampire fangs, decorating the apartment, and buying what Shawn claimed was *way too much* candy for the trick-or-treaters. To Shawn's relief, it was just Halloween that Ethan was so fond of. "It's getting ridiculous."

"Bah humbug," Shawn repeated. Sophia chuckled and shook her head. "You laugh. I walked into Kohl's the other day, and they had a sign up that had a *countdown to Christmas* on it. My first reaction was to kick it."

Ethan laughed. "Well, at least he didn't actually do it."

Sophia held up her glass, almost mockingly. "To learning some damn restraint."

"I love you too, Soph," Shawn replied, clinking their glasses together anyway. Their shared amusement was clear as they smiled, eyeing each other over their drinks.

"Don't encourage him, Fia," Ethan spoke, using the nickname he'd saddled her with almost immediately. "I'd like to make it through Christmas without having to bail him out for an assault on a Santa Claus."

"I'm not that bad!" Shawn defended. Neither of his dinner companions were listening, too busy laughing at his expense.

CHAPTER THIRTEEN

Rain rolled off the roof, making a soft *tink* as it hit the gutters, a calming white noise in the early morning hours. Despite that, Ethan was awake. He was lying on his side, gazing over at his lover. Shawn was on his back, one leg dangling off the side of the bed. A hand was on his bare abdomen, the sheets having pooled around his waist sometime in the night. The other arm was reaching toward Ethan, and he threaded their fingers together as he propped himself up on his elbow.

There was no helping the look of utter adoration that came across Ethan's face gazing at Shawn's sleeping form. Shawn was something akin to a big puppy when he was out like a light. His features softened out, whatever stress Shawn had undoubtedly dealt with that day melting away with ease. The man claimed it had something to do with Ethan's presence. Though Ethan had his doubts, the sentiment made him smile all the same.

Letting go of his hand, Ethan brought his own up to comb through Shawn's curly hair. It was times like these that Ethan was certain he had found all he was waiting for.

Shawn stirred, eyes blinking open. Lidded blue-gray orbs gazed up at Ethan, and it took Shawn a bit before he processed who he was seeing. "Hey," he spoke, his voice rough with sleep.

"Hey," Ethan greeted with an amused little smile. "Shouldn't you be sleeping?"

Stretching out, Shawn groaned in a mix of pain and pleasure, sighing when he relaxed once again into the mattress. "Shouldn't you?" he shot back, a smile on his face. Shawn rolled his body up, stealing a kiss from Ethan before he could respond.

Ethan shook his head. "Get ready for work. I'll go make breakfast."

Shawn begrudgingly agreed, leaning against Ethan to kiss more. He grumbled a complaint when Ethan eventually shooed him away though. Not that Ethan really wanted to get out of bed either; however, there was work to be done.

Showered and dressed, Shawn was greeted with a big glass of orange juice and a simple ham-and-cheese omelet. It brought a fond smile to Shawn's face all the same. Ethan was proud to have put Shawn's little cooking lessons to good use, even if Ethan pretended otherwise sometimes.

"Don't stay too long, yeah?" Ethan prompted when he walked Shawn to the door. Shawn reassured him with a smile and a kiss, Ethan watching from the doorway until the car was out of sight.

Grinning with intent, Ethan shot a quick text off to Sophia, and then he went into the kitchen to clean up the remains of breakfast. He also called the ranch.

"Happy Thanksgiving, Mom," Ethan greeted, phone on speaker where it sat on the countertop as he ran water in the sink.

"Ethan! Happy Thanksgiving. You're up early."

Admittedly she had a point. He had been spoiled by being away from home. If he didn't need to get up early, then he took advantage and usually slept in until late morning. "Got up to see Shawn off." Deciding to cut to the chase of the main reason he was calling, he asked, "Are Dad and Matty there?"

"Your dad's here and Matt..." She paused. "Looks like he just got in from the barn. Let me put you on speaker."

"Yo, bro!" Matt called, clearly coming into the room. "Happy Thanksgiving."

With holiday greetings exchanged all around, Ethan got to the point. "Would it be okay if I brought Shawn home with me for Christmas?"

There was an understandable pause. Matt had known about Shawn longer; however, his parents probably knew more about him as a person. It was the curse of a parent, Ethan figured, having pried plenty of information about Shawn from him. Although Ethan refused to betray his boyfriend's trust by talking about any topics that were too personal— Shawn could do that himself if he chose to.

Aileen asked reasonably, "Shouldn't he be with his family for Christmas?"

"There's, uh..." Ethan shifted uncomfortably. "It's complicated." He didn't really want to get into the details, especially on a holiday.

Surprisingly enough, it was Henry who answered, "Of course he can come, kiddo."

"Yeah?" Ethan felt a weight lift off his shoulders. Even though he'd told Shawn his parents wouldn't mind, he was still nervous about asking.

"We'd love to have him," Aileen assured him, the smile clear in her voice.

They weren't just saying it to make him happy; that much was certain, and Ethan felt his chest swell. It probably doubled when Matt threw in, "Hope he knows what he's getting into."

"I'm not sure much could prepare someone for a Brant-family Christmas."

* * *

Ethan had the long weekend off for Thanksgiving, and despite Shawn believing he should have been with his family, Ethan had insisted they would wait until he took his vacation over Christmas. Shawn had never been one for holidays. Still, he told Ethan they could grab some dinner after he got off work.

Ethan didn't seem to mind, although Shawn had his doubts. Ethan was used to being with his family, a relationship Shawn had never experienced with his own parents. Shawn knew it had to be hard on Ethan being away from home at times like this, so he would try to at least *pretend* to enjoy himself.

Despite his plan to take a half day, Shawn got caught up in paperwork, and it wasn't until Davies kicked his chair that he realized it was already four. "Go the fuck home already, Greyson," he griped, putting on his coat.

"Going to your folks'?" Shawn inquired, for once not arguing about leaving work as he stood to gather his things.

"Yup. Time to go stuff myself stupid." Davies grinned. If there was one thing the guy could do, it was eat. They had gone out for enough meals over the years for Shawn to know how much he could put away; Davies's metabolism was something else.

"Better bring me one of your Gran's pies," Shawn reminded him as they were walking out. The Davies matriarch's cran-raspberry pie was amazing. She always baked extra for Davies to bring to the station during the holidays, and Shawn wasn't above bribing for one all his own.

"Just remember you owe me those pecan things, and we'll call it even."

"Deal." The next time Shawn got into a baking mood he would have to make more of the pecan clusters Davies seemed to favor, particularly the white-chocolate ones.

They parted ways in the parking garage. "Hey, Shawn." Shawn paused, looking at Davies. "Happy Thanksgiving."

Shawn somehow managed a smile. "Yeah. You too."

He supposed there was at least one good thing to be happy about today, and it was waiting at home for him.

* * *

When he walked in the door, Shawn received a surprise. "Soph?" His sister and Ethan were standing in the kitchen, surrounded by platters and bowls of food, a half-carved turkey out on the counter.

"Uh..." Ethan looked a little guilty. "Welcome home?"

Shawn burst out laughing, walking in to give them both hugs. "Seriously? You guys planned this?"

"Texted Davies when the turkey was almost done," Ethan informed him with a smirk, arm still wrapped around Shawn's waist.

"We invited him to join us," Sophia said, "but he said he was already booked."

"Gave us a raincheck," Ethan added. Shawn knew what that meant— drinks at O'Connell's, a downtown pub the detectives had decided was a good hangout.

Despite not caring for holidays, Shawn couldn't help but smile. He was so grateful to have Ethan and Sophia in his life.

Sentimentality aside, Shawn did manage to have a good time. Still, he was glad when his sister left, and the house was quiet again.

Shawn finished up in the kitchen, where he had chased the pair away earlier, insisting on storing the leftovers himself. Dishwasher loaded and roaster soaking in the sink, Shawn went into the living room. He smiled softly at the sight that greeted him.

A small fire was crackling away in the fireplace, despite the weather still being above freezing at night. The music playing softly through the stereo speakers was an old jazz tune he'd turned Ethan onto—so much so, it had found a place on Ethan's therapy playlist. As the singer crooned, Shawn walked up behind the recliner.

Ethan was lying back, his legs brought up and bent cross-legged. His arms were resting on the sides, palms facing upward. It was hard to tell if Ethan was simply meditating or had actually drifted off to sleep. When Shawn bent over to press a soft kiss to his forehead, he got his answer.

He looked down at green eyes and a gentle smile. "Thank you," Shawn murmured, the next kiss falling at the corner of Ethan's mouth.

"Glad you enjoyed it," Ethan replied, hand coming up to snag Shawn's.

"Come on," Shawn prodded. "Let's go to bed."

Ethan hummed in appreciation. "Sounds good." As he got to his feet, he added with a smirk, "I'm just glad we didn't destroy the kitchen."

Shawn chuckled. "It's much appreciated."

Ethan bumped their hips together, and Shawn snagged him around the waist. He pulled Ethan's back against his chest. Shawn nuzzled into his hair before kissing behind Ethan's ear.

"Come on, you," Ethan urged, shuffling down the hall and pulling Shawn along with him. "You can be a cuddly, sleepy bear in bed."

Shawn only smiled against his neck.

* * *

O'Connell's was abuzz with activity. Shawn looked over at Ethan, making sure the crowd wasn't going to bother him. Ethan caught him watching, his lips twitching up a little as he swatted Shawn's hip. Ethan jerked his chin forward, indicating that he was fine.

"There's my two favorite guys," Davies crowed from his stool at the corner of the bar. "Come on." He patted the stool next to him, and Ethan slipped easily beside him. Shawn walked around the corner and then sat at Davies's other side so they could all talk better.

The bartender came over, setting a fresh Guinness Blonde in front of Davies and looking to the pair for what they wanted. "Macallan," Shawn ordered. "On the rocks."

"Do you have Maker's Mark?" Ethan asked.

The bartender nodded and went to get their drinks.

"You're both assholes," Davies said, taking a swig of his beer. "Coming to an Irish pub and ordering that shit."

"I could order wine," Shawn teased, a familiar dig between them. While he preferred wine with dinner, on the rare occasion he went out just for drinks he would indulge in a good scotch.

"Yeah, yeah." Davies waved them off. Once their drinks had been delivered, he held up his own. "Happy Holidays, guys."

Ethan offered a little smile as he clinked their glasses together. "Happy Holidays."

"Bah humbug," Shawn said as he raised his own glass, lips curled into a grin despite his comment.

It was their version of a Christmas get-together. After all, Shawn hadn't attended the department holiday party in years. And Ethan, well, he wasn't about to walk into an entire hall full of nothing but cops. He may have been doing well with his PTSD, but there was no sense in tempting fate.

Of course, as usual, fate had its own ideas.

* * *

Ethan happened to be looking at Shawn, while they were chatting idly, when Shawn's eyes widened. Turning halfway on his stool, Ethan looked toward the door to find the source. A half dozen uniformed officers had just walked in.

Turning back as fast as he did probably should have snapped Ethan's neck. The blood drained from his face, and he felt every bit a deer in the headlights when he looked to Shawn for help.

It was Davies, though, who said, "Put your earbuds in." When Ethan just looked at him, Davies held up his hands. "We won't be offended, man. Do what you gotta do."

Shawn had a forced smile, giving him an encouraging nod, so Ethan pulled out his earbuds and plugged them into his phone. He could hear the laughter growing as the officers made it over to their end of the room, tapping his playlist just as someone was greeting Davies.

Ethan couldn't hear the conversation with "Firework" playing, but boy, could he hear Sebastian laughing in his head for having *that* song on his playlist. Not that his best friend was one to talk, with his Cher obsession—he acted like "Strong Enough" was his own personal mantra.

Ethan watched as all the cops greeted Shawn and Davies like good buddies, or at the least brothers-in-arms. He also saw the questioning looks they were sending his way.

Feeling his anxiety rise, Ethan closed his eyes, putting his head down on the bar. He tried to focus on his breathing, allowing the music to wrap around him. It was a bright little cocoon he made for himself, a place just as safe as Shawn's arms.

Of course, that would be when someone tapped him on the shoulder. Ethan straightened, pulling one of his earbuds out to look at the officer. He seemed vaguely familiar though it wasn't anyone he'd ever worked with directly. "Yeah?" Perhaps a little harsh, but Ethan wasn't in a place mentally to want to talk.

The man didn't seem offended in the least. "Steve Graham," he introduced himself, going to offer his hand before thinking twice about it and pulling it back to his side. He cleared his throat. "I was Jay Wilson's partner."

Ethan stiffened momentarily before managing a little nod of acknowledgment. "Sorry 'bout—"

Steve waved it off. "Nothing to apologize for."

Of course, it wasn't Ethan's fault Jay had ultimately been let go by the department. The investigation of the shooting had turned up a few things that had worried the powers that be. Jay had acted recklessly by firing his gun, and it had nearly cost a bystander—a fellow cop—his life. That sort of negligence couldn't be overlooked. No formal charges had been filed—at Ethan's insistence—but Jay had still had to be let go as far as the board was concerned.

"I just wanted to say hey," Steve continued. "We didn't really meet before, so..."

That was putting it mildly. The last thing Ethan recalled properly was Shawn's face. Everything after that was lights and blurs and muted sound. Then he had been waking in a hospital bed, and Shawn had come in to see him.

When some officers had come to take his statement the following morning, Ethan had become so agitated that the staff had forced them to leave. It had taken a couple more attempts to figure out Ethan wasn't going to respond to them. It was only too bad Shawn couldn't have done it, but as he had been involved in the shooting, he couldn't. Finally, one of the women from Internal Affairs had shown up, and between her empathetic demeanor and business dress, Ethan had managed to get through it.

No one was surprised he hadn't shown up to the formal hearing involving Jay, especially after the official PTSD diagnosis came down.

"Sorry," Steve said, pulling Ethan from his terrible thoughts. Seeming to sense Ethan's growing unease, he simply excused himself by saying, "Glad to see you're doing better."

Ethan watched him go, joining the other officers who had since gone to grab a table in the back. He then turned to Shawn and Davies who both gave him encouraging looks. Still not feeling completely stable at the moment, Ethan nodded, returning the earbud and pillowing his head on his arms as he shut his eyes. He could only smile when he felt an arm wrap around him, giving his shoulder a squeeze, while another hand took his, threading their fingers together.

CHAPTER FOURTEEN

Ethan adjusted his tie again after he stepped out of the car. He was uncomfortable enough in a regular tie, yet there he was in a bow tie and full-on tuxedo. When Shawn had informed him it was a black-tie event, Ethan had given him a blank look. Upon finding out what that entailed, he'd told Shawn they should forget the whole thing.

Not that Sophia was allowing them to back out after Ethan had shoved his foot in his mouth. He wasn't likely to make the same mistake twice.

The gray stone mansion they stood in front of was massive. Ethan didn't understand how a family of four could even *use* that much space. He supposed it blended in with the rest of Medina, a rich and affluent Seattle suburb that sat on the other side of Lake Washington.

Shawn looked over at him in amusement after passing the keys off to the valet his parents had hired for the evening. "Nervous?"

"More like uncomfortable." He pulled at his collar a little more. "Didn't even wear a monkey suit to my prom. How do people actually *wear* these things?"

"Got me, babe." Shawn smiled at him gently, eyes filled with obvious affection. "Ready to face the music?"

"Ready as I'll ever be," Ethan mumbled. He caught the way the women in the car that had pulled up behind them looked them both over appraisingly before being escorted in by their male counterparts.

Shawn must have seen him watching as he smirked and offered his arm. "Shall we?"

With a bright laugh, Ethan slipped his arm into the crook of Shawn's elbow. "Why thank you, my good sir," Ethan replied with an airy accent, delighted at the responding chuckle it caused.

Once they stepped into the expansive foyer, Ethan felt all his nerves return. He felt as if his eyes were bulging out of his head, the opulence overwhelming. He looked to Shawn for reassurance, but Shawn was already giving a comforting squeeze to his arm.

"Mr. Greyson," a woman greeted with an obviously pleased smile. "How are you, sir? It's been too long."

Shawn's returning smile was genuine. "I've been fine, Amalia," he replied, pressing a kiss to her cheek. Shawn removed his overcoat and passed it to her, both looking at Ethan next. He apologized, hurrying to give Amalia his own coat. Shawn pressed a hand to his hip, a smile threatening to cross his face as he soothed, "Relax."

"Easy for you to say," Ethan replied quietly, gaze darting around to the other people who entered the foyer.

"Come on," Shawn encouraged. "Let's get this over with."

* * *

It wasn't as though Shawn was looking forward to it any more than Ethan was. As far as he was concerned, they were walking into the lions' den. Even so, he put on a brave face, if only for Ethan.

They entered the parlor, where his parents were holding court, greeting the guests as they arrived before joining them in the ballroom later. Sophia was standing with them, nodding along politely with whatever the current arrivals were saying. Her face lit up when she spotted Shawn and Ethan, so she quickly excused herself and rushed over.

"Thank God," she breathed, wrapping an arm around each of their necks and pulling them in. "I am way too sober for this," she whispered in their ears.

"Agreed," Shawn drawled. The guests in front of them were taking their leave, making it their turn. "Time to face the music," he added gravely.

"Shawn," his mother greeted, almost welcoming. Caroline was a petite woman, blonde and every bit as dainty in her build as she portrayed in her demeanor. She gave him a hug, albeit a bit awkwardly, and glanced over at Ethan.

"Sophia said you would be coming," his father commented. Shawn shook his hand, the pair long past attempting any kind of affection. William had been an imposing figure when Shawn was a child, but these days Shawn couldn't be intimidated by him. Sharp gray eyes, which matched Shawn's own, cut over to Ethan, and Shawn knew it was the moment of truth.

"Mom, Dad, I'd like you to meet Ethan Brant." Ethan gave a half smile as he offered his hand to William. His father took it with some trepidation, obviously fearing the next words out of Shawn's mouth. "Ethan's my new boyfriend."

Naturally, Caroline looked aghast, but quickly caught herself. Ethan didn't really give her a choice, taking her hand in his and offering a grin. "Ma'am." Shawn had to work to keep a straight face, knowing full well his boyfriend had purposefully gone a little heavy on his drawl.

Caroline was searching for something to say, and William appeared near to bursting. "Well, um, yes, it was...nice of you to come," Caroline managed while William clapped a hand on Shawn's shoulder and said in a low voice, "Would you mind coming over here a minute?"

Not having any of it, Sophia greeted the couple who arrived behind them. "Judge Simmons! Well it's just been forever, hasn't it?"

William removed his hand, giving Shawn a hard look. "We'll be talking about this later," William promised through gritted teeth.

"Whatever," Shawn muttered.

Sophia linked her arm with her brother's. "Be a dear and come get some punch with me. Did you need any, Mom?"

"What? Oh, no dear, I'm fine. Shawn?" He hesitated, looking at Caroline expectantly. "It's good to see you."

Shawn's lips twitched into the briefest of smiles as he gave her a little nod. Caroline was trying, he'd give her that, but it was too long overdue. Shawn's heart had hardened, with no hope of reconciliation, not after everything they had put him through.

"For the love of God," Sophia hissed once they were free, having slipped away into the ballroom. "I need a drink."

"And that was just the warm-up," Shawn replied dryly. "I'm sure Dad will still want to give me a lecture while Mom gets dramatic about why I have to *choose to be gay*."

That had always been a rather bitter point of contention between him and his parents. In their eyes if he was bisexual, then he could just *choose* to be with women. Shawn had never wanted to deny any part of who he was, and he wouldn't.

"What the hell did you get us into, Fia?" Ethan asked, looking around the ballroom at the vast array of people.

To avoid doing such a large formal dinner, the Greyson party was always held postsupper so as to serve hors d'oeuvres and small finger foods. A string orchestra was set up at the far end of the ballroom, some people already starting to dance.

"There's an open bar," Sophia offered, steering them in that direction.

"I'm gonna need it," Ethan concluded, tugging at his collar again.

"He does clean up well," Sophia noted, smiling over at Ethan. Then again she really should have approved, given she had gone with them to help buy the formal wear.

"Not too bad yourself." Ethan gave her a wink.

"Yeah, I'm sure Mom had a heart attack when she saw that," Shawn mentioned, referring to the red evening gown she wore that clung to every curve.

"Actually, she told me I should be showing off the assets since I'm getting old and still need to catch a husband." Sophia looked down at her cleavage pointedly. "I dunno. Think it's too much?"

Shawn shook his head. "I'm not listening to this." They had reached the bartender just in time. "Scotch on the rocks." He knew his parents would only have the best liquor on hand, so there was no need to be specific. He also knew that bourbon wasn't on the menu. "Vodka cran?" he suggested to Ethan.

Ethan scrunched his nose. "Are you high?" He looked around a moment before leaning in and stage-whispering, "If so, you've *got* to share, dude." Shawn barked out a laugh, head thrown back the way he did when he was truly happy. One glance and Shawn knew it was taking all of Ethan's willpower not to lean over and press a kiss to his throat as was becoming habit.

"Actually," Sophia informed them, "I made sure there was a stashed bottle." She asked the bartender for the bourbon and then a martini for herself. "To long nights."

Three glasses *clinked* together. A long night indeed.

* * *

Ethan found his errant boyfriend out on the terrace. Shawn had his drink in hand, leaning his forearms on the railing as he sipped at it, gazing out into the back gardens and pool area. "Hey," Ethan spoke gently, coming to the rail next to him, "there you are." He pressed their shoulders together, smiling a bit when Shawn offered him a twitch of his own lips. "What are you doing out here?"

"Thinking."

Making a humming sound, Ethan turned, half sitting on the rail as he looked back toward the ballroom. Then his gaze drifted over the exterior, which was just as decadent as the rest of the mansion. "It's a nice place," he noted.

Shawn snorted. "It's *aesthetically pleasing*. But it's not a home. Just a building people live in."

Ethan frowned, although he understood, after everything Sophia had told him and what little he'd managed to get out of Shawn on the topic of their parents. Given the reception they'd received and the reaction of the guests, well, Ethan couldn't believe his boyfriend had grown up here. Shawn had turned out so different from his parents, as had Sophia, and Ethan was even more grateful for his own family.

"Was glad to get the hell out of this," Shawn continued. "To leave it all behind."

Even though he suspected the answer, Ethan felt the need to ask, "Don't you have *any* good memories of growing up?"

Shawn shrugged. He straightened and turned to lean back against the rail. "Can't say I have many. My parents were always so worried about appearances and their reputations that they never really took the time to actually be *parents* at all. Outside of the time I spent with my sister, most of my *good* memories are things I did on my own."

"That's rough," Ethan murmured, looking at his feet.

"I've dealt with it" was Shawn's detached reply. "I live for me now. Not them."

Ethan's hand found his, linking their fingers together in comfort.

They stood there in thoughtful silence for a time before Shawn gave a short humorless laugh. "I remember how furious they were when I said I was leaving law school to become a cop. They even threatened to take me out of their wills."

Ethan smirked. "I can imagine your response to that."

"Actually it wouldn't be what you'd expect."

Ethan tilted his head.

"I stayed in school for another year. Wasn't until Soph convinced me to do what *I* wanted that I actually did it."

"Really?" Ethan could barely believe that. He had always known Shawn to be so confident.

"Like I said, that's not who I am anymore." He gave a shrug. "It took a lot of coaxing from Sophia to get me out of my shell. She's always been there for me, pushing me, wanting me to be happy."

Ethan had picked up on that from their time hanging out with Sophia. Now he was imagining a slightly more resigned Shawn looking up to his big sister. Ethan knew what it was like being an older sibling, attempting to guide the younger. Ethan only hoped he could encourage Matt half as much as Sophia did for Shawn.

"I just wanted to make them proud," Shawn continued. "Especially after disappointing them when I came out." He huffed, shaking his head as he pushed away from the rail. "'Course that's not how I see things anymore." He met Ethan's gaze. "To hell with them. There's nothing wrong with me."

Ethan offered him a loving smile, moving to stand toe to toe with him. "You're perfect just the way you are."

Shawn gave him a little smile in turn, his hand resting on Ethan's hip as he lowered his forehead to Ethan's. "Thank you," Shawn breathed out, his eyes falling shut. A hand came up to rest on the back of Shawn's neck, grounding him and reminding him that he had a support net in Ethan.

After a few moments of simply standing there, gaining strength from each other, Ethan suggested, "Let's go back in and get this over with. Fia said we'd only have to stay like an hour more before we could run for the hills."

"I am so holding her to that."

* * *

When they walked back into the ballroom, it seemed everyone had arrived as Shawn's parents were mingling with the people who weren't dancing. After watching the couples spinning around on the floor, Shawn grinned, looking over at Ethan. "I don't like that look," Ethan mentioned.

"If you and Sophia got me into this, then I'm at least getting a dance out of it."

Shawn tugged him toward the floor, Ethan protesting the whole way. "I don't know how to dance!" he hissed. "Not like this!"

"I'll lead. It'll be fine."

Ethan looked at him skeptically, even as Shawn was joining their hands together and placing Ethan's other hand on his shoulder. "Shawn, I can't—"

"*Relax.*"

Sighing, Ethan gave in. He liked to dance—that wasn't it—but he had no idea how to do something as formal as what he saw the other people around them doing. All of that was forgotten as Shawn started to move, forcing him into following his lead.

It was a bit stiff at first; Ethan focused mainly on his feet. Shawn tipped his chin up, giving him a little smile. "Just look up here," he encouraged. After that, Ethan found he was able to move with the rhythm, anticipating the movement of the simple step Shawn kept repeating. "There." Shawn beamed at him. "I told you that you could do it."

Ethan smiled back even though he was shaking his head. "I'm pretty sure it's jus' you makin' me look good."

"Well, there is that." Shawn laughed as Ethan squeezed his arm in protest from where it slid down from Shawn's shoulder. When Shawn pulled them a little closer together, there was no missing his smile. Shawn leaned in conspiratorially and mentioned, "Every single woman in this room is completely jealous of you right now."

Ethan scoffed, rolling his eyes. "Yeah, right."

"It's true," Shawn insisted, sweeping him into a new step that Ethan barely managed to follow without tripping over his own feet. "And all of their mothers are lamenting about how such 'good breeding' is being wasted. And my parents? Well, they're about ready to have heart attacks."

Shawn wasn't even looking anywhere but at Ethan. All the same, Ethan amused him once they fell into that familiar pattern, taking the opportunity to look around. To his shock, everything that Shawn described was absolutely true. All the young women were either pouting or glaring, while the older women openly disapproved, making undoubtedly snide comments to each other.

When he found Shawn's mother off gossiping with a circle of people, Caroline appeared about ready to faint, a hand on her chest. It was harder to find William in the crowd, but eventually, Ethan caught sight of him at the bar, downing his drink before getting another refill.

"*That* is just freaky," Ethan concluded, looking back to find Shawn smirking.

"Cutting in," a feminine voice interrupted. Sophia hip-checked her brother out of the way once they stopped. She grinned at Shawn who gave her a faux-exasperated look.

"I don't really know what I'm doing," Ethan confessed. He had just gotten used to being led, after all; now he was being asked to do everything in the opposite direction.

"Good luck," Shawn offered, with a pat on the back, smirking as he headed to grab another drink, Ethan's cursing following after him.

* * *

Before Shawn could make it to the bar, a woman he vaguely recognized stepped in his path. She gave him a fake, if not brilliant, smile. "Shawn, it's been too long. Since you're finally free of the play toy, we should catch up."

Shawn's smile had teeth and was anything but friendly as he stepped up to her. "You're not even fit to be a plaything."

Apparently the dancing was a failure because his sister and Ethan showed up at his side moments later, drawing his attention. "Your boyfriend needs more practice," Sophia griped, leaning on Ethan as she drew her foot up and rubbed it pointedly.

"Sorry, Fia," he apologized, cheeks flushing a little in embarrassment.

Shawn couldn't help but think he was the cutest thing. He reached out and pulled Ethan into a tender kiss, smiling as they parted. "You're perfect just the way you are," he assured him, echoing Ethan's earlier words.

The girl who had tried to get into Shawn's pants was thoroughly scandalized by the display, leaving in a huff.

Not seeming to notice, Ethan laughed at the comment. "I can dance much better if we just drop all of this formal crap."

"I'm game," Sophia replied, looping her arms with both of theirs.

Shawn grinned. "How about we get the hell out of here then?"

Sophia's heels were off before the valets even had Shawn's car pulled around. None of them had bothered to say good-bye to William and Caroline, but it was probably for the best. Sophia sat forward, leaning between the front seats. "Now, how about a club?"

"I know just the place," Ethan replied with a grin. An address was placed into Shawn's GPS with the plan of stopping at both siblings' homes for a change of clothes on the way—Ethan having practically half his wardrobe at Shawn's by then.

Ethan yanked his tie off and tossed it back at Sophia. He sent a mass text out to Davies and his parkour buddies. If they were going to party, they may as well do it right—straight until dawn.

CHAPTER FIFTEEN

His cell phone rang, and Ethan stopped what he was doing to answer it. The name *Davies* glowed on the screen, along with a picture of Davies holding up his middle finger to the camera. It made Ethan smile.

"Hey," Ethan greeted. "Miss me already?" It was the first week Ethan was on his new schedule of only every Friday at the station. "Y'know, it's okay if yo—"

"Brant." The sharp way Davies said his name made Ethan freeze. "It's Greyson."

"What's wrong?" Ethan rose to his feet, shutting down his computer.

"He's alright. But we're at Sacred Heart."

"I'll be right there!" Ethan felt panic bubbling up inside of him at the very idea Shawn was in a hospital. He grabbed his bag, slipping his laptop inside before reaching for his jacket.

"Let me send a car over."

"No!" Ethan didn't even want to think about dealing with a patrolman.

"Everett and Jones are in the area," Davies immediately assured him. The pair of detectives were people he'd come to know. Despite that, Ethan didn't think he could handle them, not even Jones's soft way of dealing with him.

"I'll get a cab," Ethan assured him. He hadn't noticed he was shaking until it came out in his voice.

Davies's question was gentle. "Are you sure?"

"Yeah." Ethan cleared his throat. "Yeah. I'm on my way." He was already out his office door, bag in hand.

"Okay. I'll meet you in the main lobby."

Ethan hung up and slipped his phone into his pocket and knocking on his boss's open door to grab his attention.

"Ethan?" Frank's brows lowered in concern. "Everything alright?"

Ethan shook his head, shifting from foot to foot. "I need to go."

"Whatever you need. You know that."

Ethan nodded. He didn't have to tell Frank the rest, but after all the man had done for him, and how considerate he'd been of Ethan's episodes, he felt it necessary to clarify. "Shawn's been hurt. He's at the hospital."

"What happened?"

"I dunno." Ethan ran a hand through his hair. "I just got told to come."

Frank nodded in understanding. "Keep me posted. I can have Luke cover your clients if..."

He drifted off when Ethan waved his hand. "I just need the day."

After a few parting words, Ethan hustled down the hall, drawing the strap of his messenger bag over his head to drape across his chest. He wasn't even aware of the time it took to get down the elevator and out to the curb where he flagged a taxi down.

"Sacred Heart Hospital," Ethan told the driver, vocal cords tightening.

Seated, without anything to do, fear started to creep back into his mind. Panic bubbled to the surface, and Ethan scrunched his eyes tightly while he reminded himself to breathe. He frantically dug into his pocket to pull out his phone and earbuds.

Putting them in, Ethan pulled up his playlist and just hit play. Rascal Flatts filled his head, partway through their song "Stand." He heaved a sigh, leaning back against the surprisingly comfortable seat. Breathing deeply and slowly, he let the music surround him.

Outside, there was snow and the bustle of a downtown afternoon. Inside the cab, he could pretend he wasn't quietly freaking out about all the possibilities swimming through his head.

His hand was shaking as "It's Time" started to play. He clenched his hand a moment before stretching his fingers out. Anything to stop thinking.

Ethan hadn't opened his eyes once to check on their progress, so he had no clue this particular halt in motion was his destination. "Hey kid, we're here," the grizzled old cabby snapped. Ethan jumped, yanking his earbuds out. They were, in fact, at the hospital drop-off.

"Sorry," Ethan muttered quickly, grabbing his wallet.

As Ethan passed over the fare money, the driver softened. "I hope everything's alright."

Ethan let out a little breath. "Yeah. Me too."

He stepped out into the biting cold, the wind kicking up swirls of snow. Ducking his face into his jacket, Ethan hurried for the revolving doors.

Inside, he shook the snow off as best he could while looking around the lobby. "Ethan." His heart stopped a little, head whipping around to find Davies.

Rushing to meet him halfway, Ethan demanded, "What happened? Is he alright?"

"Relax." Davies grabbed Ethan's biceps. "He's fine. Nothing major. I promise." Ethan's muscles loosened, Davies giving his arms a comforting squeeze in response. "Come on. We should be able to go back and see him."

"What happened?" Ethan repeated, scrambling to catch up with Davies's long strides.

"It's my fault," Davies grumbled. "I'm sorry."

Ethan's brows lowered. "Your fault?"

"Shouldn't have let those punks get the drop on us. I *knew* they were going to try something. I just—" Davies puffed his lips out in frustration, halting their progress down the hall toward the ER. "It was a rookie mistake."

"That what Shawn says?"

"Of course not. At the moment, he's cursing his own stupidity." Davies's lips twitched. "Which, really, he should be. Part of it's still his own fault."

Ethan raised a challenging brow.

"We were doing some *interviews* with these punks who looked like wannabe bangers. Figured they saw something. Except one of 'em pulled a knife. Your idiot boyfriend put his arm up as a shield and took it right across the arm."

Ethan bit his lip.

Davies kept on as though he didn't notice. "Well, it was on then. Many an ass was kicked. And then Princess bitched and whined the whole way here."

That had Ethan smiling despite the situation. "So nothing serious then?" It was more to reassure himself as they started walking again.

"Stitches. And probably a concussion." Davies smirked over at him. "Always told him he couldn't box for shit."

"What about you?" Ethan checked.

"I'm fine."

Ethan's eyed flicked to the cut on Davies's lip. "Looks like you could use a few stitches yourself."

"Shouldn't you be worried about your dumbass?"

"You'd have to specify. You're both dumbasses."

"Oh, that's the last time I'm nice to you," Davies declared in mock indignation.

Ethan laughed, not even worried in the least. "You love me."

"I have better taste than that."

Ethan smacked him in the back of the head.

* * *

Shawn thanked his nurse for the water. He *tsked* at himself for reaching with his right hand automatically, switching to take it with his left. "I'll be back to cover that for you in a minute," Natalie said, gesturing to the stitches.

Sighing, Shawn looked down at the red and inflamed skin stitched back together again. What had he been thinking, holding up his arm like that? *Better than your face*, he reminded himself.

The kid had pulled a butterfly knife, the flash catching Shawn's attention. It had been a reaction, nothing more, to hold his arm up as a shield. The bite of metal through flesh was something of a new experience, and one Shawn didn't want to repeat.

He supposed he was lucky that his trench coat had impeded the blade, or he would be looking at more than just stitches. As it was, the wound was rather shallow and roughly four inches long across the width of the meaty part of his forearm. Shawn would take that over the alternative.

"Shawn!" He barely had the chance to look up, before Ethan slammed into him, almost knocking him back onto the bed where he sat on the edge.

Shawn held him in return automatically, a smile gracing his face a moment. When Shawn spotted Davies in the doorway, he glared. "I told you I'd call him."

Davies smirked, coming inside to lean against the wall. "Oh, I was not letting you get out of this one, Greyson."

"Asshole," Shawn muttered.

Ethan pulled away, glowering down at him. "I'd hit you right now if you didn't have a concussion."

Shawn winced at the thought. "Please don't. My head hurts enough as is."

Ethan's hackles lowered. "You gonna be alright?"

Offering him a smile, he reached out and took Ethan's hand. "'Course. Takes more than a little scuffle to knock me out."

"Detective," Doctor Sun greeted when he walked in. "The CT came back good. No major brain trauma."

"Test 'im again, Doc," Davies commented.

"Shut it, smartass," Shawn groused back.

Doctor Sun appeared to be holding back a grin. "You still have a concussion, even if it is minor. That means plenty of rest, no exertion, no alcohol—"

"Not my first one," Shawn interrupted. "I know the drill."

"I want you taking it easy this week. You should feel fine again within a couple days, but you need to watch." He paused to look at Shawn's chart. "I'd recommend staying overnight—" Shawn scoffed and Doctor Sun smiled. "*But,* as long as someone can stay with you, then I'm alright with releasing you."

"I'll be with him," Ethan said quickly, grabbing Shawn's left hand and giving it a squeeze.

"Very good. Make sure he takes it easy. It's fine for him to sleep, but wake him every two hours. Ask him a few questions—date, birthday, who's the President—"

"An asshole," Shawn and Davies droned simultaneously.

"Ice packs for his head if he needs them," Doctor Sun continued undeterred. "If the pain worsens or he has any other symptoms that pop up, call us."

"Will do," Ethan assured her, sending Shawn a look that clearly meant he wasn't allowed to argue.

Doctor Sun nodded. "Good. I'll have your discharge packet put together, and once Natalie wraps that arm, you'll be alright to leave. You'll need to set up an appointment with your primary doctor in a couple of days. They'll be able to clear you to return to work. Any questions?"

"I think we've got it," Ethan replied. "Thanks."

Once the doctor left, Davies piped up, right on cue. "Fifty bucks says he doesn't make it a day."

"I'm *fine*," Shawn insisted. "My head just got a little rattled. You heard him. There's nothing wrong."

Ethan was frowning as he picked up Shawn's injured arm. "I wouldn't call this nothing."

Shawn huffed air from his nose as he deflated. "I didn't want to worry you."

"Idiot." Ethan shook his head. "I'll always worry about you."

Shawn accepted the gentle verbal chastising. Honestly, he had expected much worse.

Had Davies not been canvassing the scene with him, well, it could have been a completely different phone call. As it was, Davies had been at his back. Between the two of them, it hadn't been all that difficult to get the situation back under control, even with it being six on two.

Then again, seeing two of their friends go down with Tasers, another with a broken wrist, and yet someone else with a broken nose, it wasn't a stretch that they had all cooperated rather quickly after that.

"Least I didn't need a tetanus shot on top of it," Shawn mused.

Ethan went to smack him and only barely held back.

* * *

It was nearing nightfall by the time they got to Shawn's house. Davies had driven them to the station—grumbling about how he better not find blood in his car—where Ethan picked up Shawn's car and drove them home. After tossing the keys on the little table inside the door, Ethan shrugged out of his jacket and helped Shawn with his before putting them both in the hall closet.

"You sit."

Shawn grunted.

"I know this is gonna be hard on you," Ethan said. "You ain't exactly one for relaxin' or stayin' put, but yer gonna have to, so suck it up."

Shawn muttered to himself as he was forced into the living room. "Pushy pain in my ass."

"Now sit," Ethan repeated, pushing on Shawn's shoulders. "I can't throw books at you and tell you to catch up on reading, so I'm gonna order us a pizza, and we'll watch a movie."

"Doesn't sound bad," Shawn relented, getting comfortable.

"Good." Ethan leaned over the back of the couch, dropping a kiss onto the top of Shawn's head. "Stay put."

He went into the kitchen in search of the takeout menus stashed in one of the drawers. Shawn had been horrified by them, at first, but he had been made to see the perks of not having to cook every night—even if he still bitched occasionally. It was just as well that despite preferring home-cooked meals, Shawn wasn't a health nut—completely, anyway.

Pizza ordered, Ethan joined Shawn in the living room, where he was flipping through Netflix. "What did you have in mind?" Shawn asked.

"A comedy?" Ethan suggested. "Something light that you don't have to think about. And nothing that would come with a seizure warning."

Shawn's lips turned up at the corner. "Yes, mother."

"Hey," Ethan defended, "I've had a concussion before. I know it sucks, but humor me, hmm?"

He had Shawn's full attention then. "When'd that happen?"

"Shit, I was in high school. Got thrown off one of the horses and smacked my head. Lucky I didn't split it open. Mom about flipped." Ethan thought about it. "Actually, I take that back. She flipped." Shawn chuckled, and Ethan gave him a little smile. "So yes, I know how it is. If you're lucky, you'll be able to sleep."

Shawn nodded. "I slept a lot last time I had one."

"Which would have been?"

Shawn furrowed his brows trying to remember. "About three years ago now? Got into an altercation with a suspect."

"You've apparently got a knack for it."

Shawn's laugh that time was a little lighter, more relaxed.

Ethan reached over and ran his thumb across Shawn's cheek, passing under the mark at his temple. Color was already blossoming there and was bound to worsen before it got better. "Hope that heals before we head to my parents'," he mused. "Wouldn't want 'em to think you're a troublemaker, now would we?"

Shawn's grin was bright. He leaned over to give Ethan a kiss. "I thought you had a thing for bad boys?" he teased.

"I told you that in confidence, you know," he joked right back.

Shawn gave him another kiss. "Promise to keep it to myself."

Ethan wrapped him up, pulling him in tightly. "You had me so worried, y' know," he murmured. "I thought I was gonna lose my mind."

Shawn squeezed him in return. "I'm sorry."

"'S okay." Ethan sniffed, refusing to cry about what could have been. "Just got scared is all. You're the best thing that's ever happened to me. And if you were gone...?"

Shawn took Ethan's face in his hands as he pulled back. "Not going anywhere."

That time, it was Ethan's turn to steal a kiss, long and slowly, reminding himself Shawn really was alive and whole. "Don't scare me like that again."

"Can't promise that," Shawn replied. "But I swear I'll do my best."

Ethan smiled. "That'll have to do then."

Ethan readjusted them so he was pressed into the corner of the couch, legs stretched out and bracketing Shawn, who leaned back against him.

"Ah, I've got the perfect movie," Ethan said once they were settled. He took the remote from Shawn and started to type in the title.

"Seriously?" Shawn laughed when he saw what it was.

"You've seen it?" Ethan was actually surprised by that.

"Sophia had me watch it with her when I was...sixteen? I think she was attempting to be supportive."

Ethan grinned. "Sebby and I would watch it whenever we needed cheering up. Matty used to watch it with me too."

Shawn smiled at him upside down as he snuggled closer. "*Birdcage* it is then."

Ethan hit play.

CHAPTER SIXTEEN

They were on a road trip to the Brant-family ranch. According to Ethan, their property backed a national forest. The county was all agricultural land, the location of the ranch itself within the boundaries of Silver Creek—so named for the profitable mining back during the time of the rush out West.

The small town was south of Missoula, nestled between two mountain ranges. The Bitterroot River ran right through town, feeding the creeks and streams that helped all the ranches flourish. Sweetwater Ranch was a smaller operation than most, but Ethan's folks had always preferred to keep it that way, creating minimum need for outside help.

They were pulling into the center of town when Shawn was struck by a strange feeling. The first word that came to mind was quaint. It was picturesque with small businesses on either side of the double-lane paved road. Like stepping back in time, there were antique-looking black light poles and almost Old West–styled facades on the buildings. Festive decorations of wreaths and colored lights dotting the structures were strung across the road.

His observations were cut short when Ethan instructed him to pull over. Shawn parked in front of what appeared to be a small grocery store and Ethan explained, "Wanna grab a few things and figure I should drive from here."

"I could use a break," Shawn admitted, "but didn't think it was that much farther."

"It's not," Ethan replied as they got out of the car, raising his voice a little to call over, "But you'd probably lose a tire on those back roads." Ethan chuckled while Shawn shook his head, shoving his hands farther into his jacket pockets.

They met on the sidewalk that was cleared and covered in salt, when another couple came out of the store. After one glance at Ethan, the woman called his name in excitement. "Well, look at this stranger!" she crowed, practically pouncing on Ethan for a hug. She was a petite little thing who Ethan was easily able to pick up, her long blonde hair blowing in the wind.

"Hey, man!" the guy added, a pleasant smile on his face as he traded a fist bump with Ethan. He was built like a jock, Shawn noted, all muscle and tall. "Back for Christmas?"

"Yeah." Ethan followed their gazes to Shawn, smiling as he introduced them, "Bree, Jack, this is my boyfriend, Shawn."

"Good to meet you," Jack said, offering the hand that was free, the other holding their few plastic shopping bags.

As Shawn accepted, Ethan added, "I graduated with these two lovebirds." He smiled down at Bree, arm around her shoulders as he shook her a little bit. "Ma told me you two are finally tying the knot."

"Sometime in the spring, we think," Bree confirmed. "You *will* come, won't you? You know y'all are invited."

"'Course."

She smirked and leaned in conspiratorially, although her words were loud enough for everyone to hear. "And you can bring your cute new boyfriend too."

Shawn gave Ethan a smug grin. "Cute, see," he teased, nudging Ethan's shoulder. "Told ya I was a catch."

Ethan groaned dramatically. "*Bree*," he whined. "Now it's gone to his head, and he's gonna be incorrigible the rest of the night."

"Then my job is done."

"Yeah, making my life miserable." Ethan gave Jack a grin as he added, "Though won't be my problem much longer from the sounds of it."

Jack grimaced. "Don't remind me." Jack received a faux scoff and backhand to his chest from Bree, putting a smile on his face. "Well, her folks are expecting us back. Good seeing you again. Shouldn't be such a stranger."

"Yeah, if you're gonna be in town a while," Bree added, "we should hit up Horseshoe one night."

"I'm up for that," Ethan agreed.

Once they all said their good-byes, Shawn and Ethan slipped into the store, the small bell above it *tinkling*. Shawn prompted, "Horseshoe?"

"It's a bar right up the street. I figured we'd end up going anyway if Matty has a gig."

"Oh, that's where his band plays?" Shawn surmised. He followed behind Ethan, who had a basket in his hand, grabbing junk food as he passed by. Shawn didn't hold back his eye roll as he commented, "I hope your mother has *real* food at the house. Or do I need to pick up ingredients?"

Ethan chuckled, looking over his shoulder. "Don't worry, Gordon Ramsay; I'm sure you'll like the kitchen."

"I'm laughing hysterically on the inside," Shawn said dryly.

Ignoring the snark, Ethan answered his original question. "Yeah, Matty wasn't sure if they would be playing any gigs while we were here. Somethin' about their drummer having his arm in a cast."

While Ethan's head was in one of the refrigeration units, grabbing some frozen pizza bites, Shawn snuck the snack cakes and one of the bags of chips out of the cart to stash back on a shelf. Getting Ethan to cut down on the junk food was a challenge Shawn was working at one step at a time.

* * *

The sun was dipping lower in the sky when they finally made it to the ranch. They turned into the long drive, passing beneath the arch with the name *Sweetwater Ranch* carved on the attached wooden sign. The fields they passed were dotted with horses that had been turned out during the mild weather.

Shawn let out a long, low whistle as the house came into view. It was what he would expect of a country home. A two-story with white shake siding and gray roofing, there was a wraparound porch that held a glider and an array of rocking chairs on it. The faded red barn off to the side only added to the image.

"Ethan!" The screen door on the porch clattered shut, and Matt cleared the steps in one leap. Ethan had barely made it out of the car before he was slammed against it, gripped tightly in his brother's arms. "You made it."

"'Course I did," Ethan answered fondly, holding him just as firmly.

Turning to Shawn, Matt gave him an equally enthusiastic greeting. "Good to finally meet you, dude."

"Same," Shawn assured him, patting the young man's back before parting. He had sat in on a few of the brothers' Skype conversations, but mostly Shawn let them be, wanting to give them privacy. It was enough to get to know Matt better, and he honestly had been looking forward to hanging around the kid when they visited.

Aileen came out onto the covered porch to greet them, Henry appearing in the doorway behind her. Ethan's green eyes were easy to pick out on Aileen, a rather tall woman with a fading tan and light-brown hair pulled back in a ponytail. There was no mistaking Henry as anyone but Ethan's father either. He was a perfectly older version with graying hair and a few wrinkles on his rugged face, looking every bit the classic cowboy all the way down to his boots.

"Shawn," Henry greeted while his wife hugged and fussed over Ethan the second he stepped on the porch. "Welcome to Sweetwater Ranch. Good to have ya here."

Shawn accepted Henry's hand, a bit taken aback by such a hospitable greeting. "Thanks...I, uh...I'm glad to be here." Somehow he managed to smile, even rooted as he was on the stairs.

"Ma, come on," Ethan complained. "I'm gonna be here over a week. I ain't runnin' out the door."

"Hush, you," she scolded, though there was no heat to it. She swatted at Ethan as she pulled away, gaze going over to Shawn, who managed to get up the last couple of steps.

"Mom, this is Shawn Greyson."

"Come here, dear," Aileen spoke, welcoming him, literally, with open arms. The hug took him even more by surprise than the handshake had. "Good to finally meet you." She rubbed his back, chin on his shoulder.

Catching himself, Shawn let out a little huff of a laugh and managed to hug her back. "Good to be here," he replied, eyes falling shut in contentment.

* * *

Walking downstairs the next morning, Ethan chuckled when he found Shawn alongside Aileen in the kitchen. Padding over in bare feet, Ethan pressed against Shawn's back and kissed his jaw. "Yer up early." Ethan's voice was a little rough from just waking up himself.

"Asked your mom last night what time breakfast was served so I could help."

"I'm stealing him," Aileen announced, moving the bacon around in the pan. That was a smell sure to rouse Matt from sleep and would wake his father too if Ethan didn't know he was already up and out in the barn feeding the animals.

"Can't keep 'im," Ethan replied, leaning over Shawn to poke his finger into the pancake batter he was whipping up. "He's mine." Shawn shook his head but returned the soft kiss Ethan gave him before heading for the fridge.

"You couldn't even put on a shirt?" Aileen scolded. "And use a glass." She headed off before Ethan even opened the orange juice container.

Ethan trudged over to grab a glass, scratching at his stomach. "Not like we're having company," he reasoned. He was quite comfortable in just his pajama bottoms, and he knew Shawn was certainly used to it by now. Shawn, on the other hand, had at least put on sweatpants and a plain white undershirt before coming downstairs.

"You're hopeless." Aileen swatted Ethan on the backside with the spatula as he passed by.

"But you love me," Ethan replied with a cheeky grin, leaning over to kiss her cheek and hopping away before she could smack him again.

Footsteps *plopped* on the stairs as Matt trudged down, a perfect mirror of his older brother, wearing only pajama bottoms. Naturally, that caused their mother to roll her eyes and mutter under her breath about how she had two inconsiderate boys.

"I smell bacon," Matt announced the obvious.

"Help your brother set the table, and we'll eat" was Aileen's reply.

As the pair did just that, Matt suggested, "Shawn, you should come out with me an' E to the barn after breakfast. You can meet the horses 'fore we put 'em out." As long as the weather wasn't too bad, they made it a point to turn the horses out in the pasture every day. "We should go riding while you're here too."

"Riding?" Shawn turned to him with a look that said he didn't know what to make of that suggestion. "Like, on a horse?"

"*Duh.* It'll be fun."

"I dunno that 'fun' is the right word." Shawn turned his focus back to the pancakes now on the griddle. "I've never ridden a horse before."

"We woulda never guessed."

Ethan knocked his brother upside the head.

"Oh please, like you didn't wanna say it."

"Beyond the point," Ethan muttered, trading a look with Matt.

To Shawn's relief that was when Henry came in. He shook the snow from his coat and hat before hanging them up on the hooks by the back door and then kicking his boots off. "Looks like you boys made it here just in time. It's gonna be a white Christmas after all."

Ethan watched as Henry patted Shawn's shoulder when he walked by to wash his hands in the sink. There was no missing the way every fiber of Shawn's being relaxed, a stupidly happy expression on his face that made Ethan's heart sing.

CHAPTER SEVENTEEN

Shawn couldn't remember experiencing a Christmas like this—family gathered in the living room next to a brightly lit tree and a crackling fire. Everyone was enjoying the fresh-baked cinnamon rolls and eggnog, as per Brant family tradition, while they took turns opening presents from under the tree. It was so very domestic and happy that Shawn didn't really know what to do with it all.

The Brants even went out of their way to get Shawn a gift. "We weren't really sure what to get you, but Matty told us you like to read," Aileen said. The small box held a gift card for Amazon. Shawn's lips turned up in a smile as he thanked them for the unexpected surprise.

"Just wait 'til they know you better," Ethan informed him from his seat between Shawn's legs on the floor. "You'll be opening presents forever."

"If you don't want the Keurig—" Shawn was cut off by a kiss, unable to keep from smiling against Ethan's lips. Shawn had brought a few small gifts with them for Ethan to open; however, the new Keurig he got the man was hidden away in the spare bedroom closet. Instead, he gave Ethan a picture of it. "I'll take that as another thank-you."

"And you're welcome," Ethan mused in return, holding up a present for Shawn as well.

"You already gave me enough," Shawn scolded, even as he was working at the paper.

It turned out to be a Kindle. Shawn had been on the fence about getting one, only because he was an old-fashioned sort who liked the feel of a good book in his hands. He had to admit, the idea of carrying his whole library with him had its merits though.

"I love you," Shawn murmured against Ethan's cheek, wrapping his arms around Ethan and holding him close.

As all the remaining wrapping and tissue paper was being shoved into a large, black trash bag, Shawn caught Aileen giving her husband a conspiratorial smile. It was Henry who said, "Ethan, we've got one more surprise for you."

Matt hopped up, a big grin on his face. "Get yer coat on, dude."

"What?" Ethan was obviously confused but followed suit anyway. When Shawn joined them by the door to grab his own jacket, Ethan narrowed his eyes at him. "You got anythin' to do with this?"

"Don't look at me, babe," Shawn denied, slipping an arm into its sleeve.

"This is from your father and brother," Aileen chastised, swatting at Ethan's shoulder.

"And your mom," Henry insisted.

"I just encouraged them," she countered, linking her arm with Henry's as they stepped outside.

Ethan and Shawn followed them to the lean-out on the back side of the barn where the heavy equipment was kept. Shawn had half a mind to joke that a tractor wouldn't be much use back in Cape Cascara. What they found was something entirely different.

* * *

A surprised noise left Ethan's mouth, and he froze when he came around the baler and found an Indian Scout sitting there, all shining and looking great. "How?" was all Ethan could get out. The last time he'd seen the motorcycle, it had been a pile of rust.

The motorcycle was something Ethan had picked up the summer after graduation. The plan had been to fix it up and use it to get around while away at college. That hadn't happened though. Between his lack of extra funds and running into more problems than he anticipated, the bike had been relegated to a corner of the lean-out. Now the Scout was gleaming in black and red, looking brand-new.

"You won't be able to take it with you, unfortunately," Henry apologized, arm falling around Ethan's shoulders. "But she'll be here when the weather breaks."

Ethan turned into his father's side, wrapping his arms around him. "Thank you so much!" He grasped the back of Henry's jacket, completely overwhelmed. Ethan did, however, manage to turn and grab Matt into a bear hug as well.

* * *

"Figured I could drive it out there for ya," Matt offered. "Then take a flight home."

Shawn was the one to suggest, "How about spring break? You can all come out, and spend some time with us."

"Can't," Henry replied apologetically. "We'll be too busy here."

"Oh. Yeah."

"But I can come for a bit," Matt put in. "Right, Dad?"

It was Aileen who answered, "That should be fine." She put her arm around Henry's waist, looking up at him. "We'll figure something out." It was clear to Shawn the woman didn't want to prevent her sons from spending time together, and he felt grateful for that.

"Sweet!" Matt hugged his brother again, both of them laughing happily. "Dude, you gotta see all the stuff we had to do to 'er. You'll never believe it."

As Shawn watched them chatter away happily, he was reminded he had a big sister of his own to call. Maybe he would give Davies a ring, too, or at least a text. Suddenly, he was feeling just a touch homesick.

* * *

Ethan flopped onto the couch, lying down and putting one arm behind his head as the phone rang in his ear. "Merry Christmas!" was the bright greeting he received.

Ethan grinned from ear to ear. "God, Shawn would hate you right now."

Sebastian huffed. "Well, too bad for him. Didn't anyone tell him it's the most wonderful time of the year?" He ended up singing the last bit.

"You're wearing an ugly sweater right now, aren't you?" Ethan accused

"*Guilty!*"

"Big surprise," Ethan muttered under his breath, shaking his head. "Merry Christmas," he returned belatedly. "Did you get to your parents' alright?"

"Got in late last night thanks to this snow. I think I hit one of Santa's reindeer on the way up, but other than that..."

"Thanks for the text," Ethan groused.

"Chill, *Mom*. It was late."

"Uh-huh." Ethan was smirking all the same. "I texted you when we got here," he pointed out, just to get a rise out of his best friend.

"Well, since Shawn was driving, if you hadn't, I would have put a BOLO out on his car."

Ethan laughed.

"Where *is* the other half?"

"Talkin' to Fia on the phone. Was gonna call Davies too." Ethan had decided to give Shawn some privacy in the guest room and come downstairs to make his own phone call.

Sebastian's tone was sly. "Ooo, that cute detective friend of his?"

"Yes," Ethan replied, rolling his eyes, "the very cute, very *straight* friend."

"Pshaw, you're no fun."

"Nope. I am a horrible friend. I don't know how you put up with me."

"At least that makes two of us."

"Fucker," Ethan managed through a chuckle. "When are you guys leaving?" It was no secret Sebastian was insanely excited he and his parents were spending New Year's in New York City. Ethan had been hearing about it since *July*.

"Tomorrow morning. Oh my God, can you even? Times Square. Ball drop."

"Freezing cold. Too many people. Sounds lovely."

"You're sounding like that boy of yours."

"I'm sure he and Davies are planning a spree through the neighborhood to slash the inflatable snowmen and Santas when we get home."

"I don't have bail money."

After a pause, they both burst out laughing, unable to hold it in any longer.

"Just be careful," Ethan finally said. "And check in."

"Wish you could be there too," Sebastian replied wistfully.

"Yeah, me too, Sebby. Maybe another year."

It was strange not spending at least *some* part of the holidays with Sebastian. During college, they had split their breaks between each other's homes. Once they'd graduated and Ethan had moved to Cape Cascara, they'd spent Thanksgiving together at Sebastian's apartment and switched off spending New Year's at one family home or the other.

That year's Thanksgiving had been a bust when Ethan had decided to surprise Shawn. Not as though Sebastian were lonely with the large group of friends he always hosted, but it meant that not having New

Year's together either was a bit of a sting. Still, he was happy Sebastian was finally getting out to NYC.

"Have fun," Ethan continued, smiling softly.

"I'll send you plenty of pictures," Sebastian assured him. "And we'll all get together once we're back in Washington."

"Sounds like a plan." Aileen walked into the room with a tray of hot cocoa, and he smiled at her. "Well, hey, I'm gonna let you go. Love ya, man."

"Love you too, *ka ¢a*. See you soon."

Ethan hung up, swinging his legs off the couch to sit up. He traded out his phone for a cup of cocoa, grinning at his mom. "So good to be home."

Aileen pressed a kiss to the top of his head. "Good to have you home." She called for everyone else to join them before sitting down beside Ethan.

At least Shawn was unlikely to argue with the choice of Christmas movie they always watched. The Brant men had won the argument years ago, and now—whether Aileen liked it or not—*Home Alone* was here to stay.

* * *

"So how are things going?" Aileen asked. She set a cup of coffee down in front of Ethan on the kitchen table. Despite the Brants not being big coffee drinkers, since it was winter, it was more common to find a pot on in the kitchen throughout the day.

Henry passed over his own cup for a refill before looking at Ethan. "Frankly, I'm concerned about you staying out there. I don't like you being all by yourself. Not right now."

Ethan was rather surprised by Henry's words. He had always seemed more accepting of the fact Ethan had chosen to stay in Cape Cascara to make a go of it. His mom had been a whole different story, though even Aileen had become resigned to the fact Ethan would remain stubborn on the subject.

"I'm doing good, Dad, honestly." Ethan let out a little half laugh and looked down at the mug his hands were wrapped around. "Actually it's been great. Shawn...Shawn really changed things for me."

Aileen sat across from him, a cup for Henry in one hand and another for herself. "And believe me, we've noticed." She gave him a gentle smile when he looked up at her. "It's in the way you talk about him. Or even when we're just chatting. You...you sound so much better than when you started therapy."

Henry grunted. "Y'know, I don't really put much stock in all this shrink nonsense. But I don't see why we can't just find ya one up in Missoula or somethin'."

"Shrink?"

They all turned to find Matt standing in the doorway, Shawn hovering behind him. They hadn't heard the pair come back inside. In actuality, they'd all thought that Shawn going with Matt to turn the horses out after breakfast would make the chore take longer.

Ethan sighed, forced into facing the one conversation he never wanted to have with his little brother. Hell, telling Matt he was gay was certainly less nerve-wracking. "Matty," he started, "I've been... I..."

Aileen jumped in to save him when he fumbled. "Your brother's been in therapy since the accident."

"Yeah, *physical therapy*," Matt groused, scowling as he stepped into the kitchen proper. "No one said anything about a shrink."

"Honey," Aileen attempted to placate him.

Ethan managed to find his words again. "I got diagnosed with PTSD. I've been seeing a therapist for it, but I've gotten a lot better."

"And just when were you planning on telling me?" Matt looked at them accusingly, and when he didn't get a reply, he scoffed and threw up his hands. "Well, I guess that's an answer then."

"Matty..."

Matt pushed past Shawn before they heard his boots *clomping* on the stairs.

"Oh dear." Aileen started to stand. "I should go talk to him."

"No." Ethan motioned for her to stay put, heaving a sigh as he stood with some effort. "This all started 'cause I refused to just tell him the truth. I think I owe him that much."

Shawn appeared resigned. "Need any backup?"

Ethan gave him a forced half smile. "Gotta do this one on my own." Shawn nodded his agreement, pressing a kiss to his cheek and giving his bicep a squeeze in silent support. "Thanks," Ethan murmured, going after Matt.

He rapped lightly on the door, with the back of his knuckles, before simply opening it. "Matty?" His brother sat on the bed, not looking at him as he entered. "Can we talk?"

"I dunno" was the petulant reply. "*Can* we?"

Ethan's sigh was mostly frustration that time. "Don't be like that," he chastised, although it came out sounding more like a plea. He grabbed Matt's desk chair, pulling it out and then turning it to sit on it backward to look at Matt. "Can you give me a chance to explain?" Ethan put his arms on the top of the chair and then rested his chin on them.

"You can stop the hurt-puppy look," Matt answered without even looking at him. "And yes, I know yer doin' it, and I also know you got no idea that yer doin' it." He looked up then with a little curl to his lips. "I know you, bro. Or..." Matt's face fell as he looked away to a random spot on the wall over Ethan's shoulder. "I thought I did."

Not really knowing how to reply to that, Ethan frowned and looked at the floor. "I didn't—" He sighed. "It's not that I wanted to lie to you. I hated keeping it from you."

"Then why did you?" Matt demanded, hurt plain to see.

"I was scared." Ethan's voice was small, and if Matt heard, then he didn't say a word. Rather, Matt was sitting extremely still. "I'm yer big brother. I'm supposed to protect you, y'know? If I'm...*broken*, then how am I supposed to take care of you?"

It was a long moment before Matt moved, lunging across the space between his bed and the chair to wrap his arms around Ethan's neck. "You are a dumbass sometimes," Matt chided, face turned into Ethan's neck as he tried not to cry. "You big...stupid...dumbass." He gave Ethan a squeeze before pulling away to meet his gaze. Matt's eyes were moist as he said, "You think I would think—what—less of you or something?"

Ethan brought his hand up to rest on Matt's forearm. "I didn't wanna disappoint you."

Matt huffed, shaking his head as he went in for another hug. "That wouldn't disappoint me, shithead. What disappoints me is you not havin' a little more faith in me. I know you're always goin' on about doing things yerself, but I wanna help you as much as you wanna protect me."

Sighing, Ethan relaxed into the embrace as he returned it. "You're right," he admitted.

"Well, of course I am, asshole!" When Matt rose to full height that time, his lips were twisted into a little smile. "Maybe you should listen to me more often."

"Don't get too cocky, brat," Ethan replied, smiling then as well.

There was a light rap on the doorframe. Shawn was standing there, looking a bit uncertain. "Everything okay?"

Ethan jerked his head in offer for Shawn to enter. "I think we're good. Right?" he asked Matt.

"You're off the hook for now," he relented. "But you owe me a full rundown later."

"Promise."

Shawn appeared pleased as he joined them, sitting on the bed. Matt plopped on it beside him, bouncing a little. "Menace," Shawn agreed with Ethan. He had called Matt that on several occasions when they spoke about him and even more since arriving.

"Not you too," Matt complained. He threw his arms out, falling back onto the bed with a big sigh.

"Overdramatic much?" Ethan ribbed. All he got was the middle finger in return as the older men laughed.

* * *

Shawn started to look around, having already checked out Ethan's childhood room and all the things left behind—though he was glad for the larger bed and uncluttered space of the guest room. "What's this?" Shawn's brows drew together as he leaned over to the small bookshelf next to the bed, plucking a stuffed rabbit from it.

The thing was clearly old, worn-out in places where it was practically threadbare. One of the floppy ears was ripped, and the eyes had clearly been replaced with buttons. It was well-loved, that was for certain.

Matt smiled fondly, reaching for it. "Bun-Bun is special," he declared, bringing it to his chest as he lay back down. He grabbed it under the arms, raising it up to look at. "E won him for me when we were kids."

"County Fair," Ethan added. "Spent way too much money to get the damn thing too."

Shawn was pretty surprised. "And you kept it all this time?"

"'Course. It was from E."

If Shawn had held any doubts about Ethan being Matt's world, well, those were laid to rest as he smiled down at the young man. No wonder Ethan had kept his situation to himself. Shawn would have done the same to protect the sibling he so dearly loved.

CHAPTER EIGHTEEN

The Horseshoe was the place to be on the weekends, catering to a younger clientele. It was typically loud and occasionally rowdy, but always a good time to be had. They also had the benefit of being the only live music venue in town.

It was still early when Ethan and Shawn arrived. Matt's band was getting set up, and the pair went over to the small raised stage to offer a hand. "We got it," Matt assured them. "Just be sure to keep the energy going, yeah?" he directed at Ethan. "Yer my hype man."

Ethan chuckled, offering his fist up that his brother then bumped with his own. "Will do, Matty." Their drummer, Dillon, was twirling a drumstick through the fingers of his uncasted hand. "Gonna be okay there, D?" Dillon had been Matt's best friend since the dawn of time, it seemed, so Ethan had no trouble harassing him a little.

"Don't you worry, E," he shot back, stick pointed at him. "I've got mad skills."

"Who the fuck talks like that anymore?"

"Your mom."

Ethan rolled his eyes, holding up a finger before Dillon could continue down that road. "I deal with children," he lamented to Shawn who chuckled along with them.

"You love us," Matt retorted, sticking his tongue out.

"Would you ladies get back to work?" Jen griped. She was an excellent bass player. In fact, as Ethan recalled it, the Dark Horses had been her idea—the name inspired by the bar itself.

"Didn't you miss me, Jennybean?" Ethan teased her. The young girl rolled her eyes, flipping her purple-dyed hair over her shoulder and walking away. Ethan smirked over at Shawn as he explained, "Had the biggest crush on me when she was younger."

"Yeah," Matt complained, "and I had to hear all about it."

"Where the hell's Benny?" Dillon complained of their second guitarist.

As though on cue, Benny burst through the swinging door to the employee area, guitar bag slung over his shoulder. "Sorry, sorry," he apologized, staving off his friends' complaints. "Damn car didn't wanna start again." None of them said a word as they were all young adults with junker cars. It was just the way of things.

"If you're supposed to be a country band," Shawn mentioned, "why do half of you look like punk rockers?" Ben's diagonal bangs, tipped in green, fell across one eye, and his tongue was playing with a lip ring.

"They're going through a phase," Matt replied, which earned him a middle finger from Jen. Matt wiggled his brows at her, pulling the strap of his guitar over his shoulder. "Nah, just their style. But they do bring a nice rock sound in. Goes well with the new country a lot of artists have been doin'."

"If you say so."

Ethan grinned as he tattled, "Shawn is not up on his country music."

Benny actually screeched. "Blasphemy!"

"Says the Green Day look-alike," Ethan shot back with a grin. Last he had seen them all, only Jen had the wild look. Perhaps something was going on between the pair; he'd have to ask Matt later.

More people were starting to come in, and the band had to get warmed up before their first set started, so Matt wrangled them all together for a sound check. Leaving them to it, Ethan steered Shawn toward the bar.

One of the bartenders was a guy he'd gone to school with—thankfully, one who hadn't been a total douchebag back then. At least things were pleasant enough in their interaction, easing a little of Ethan's anxiety about being back home in a local haunt. Sure he would see people who he enjoyed being around and wouldn't mind catching up with, but there were bound to be others he had no intention of speaking to again, let alone seeing.

Ethan tried to put all that from his mind. He was there for Matt, and he planned to enjoy himself.

Taking Shawn's hand, Ethan led him to the table next to the dance floor right in front of the stage. It was placed by the wall so Ethan could keep his back to it and watch the room. Besides, they had a great view of the band, even if Shawn was already muttering about his poor eardrums.

* * *

As the place started to fill up, Shawn spotted the couple they ran into that first day in town, holding up his hand to them. Bree tugged on Jack's arm, pointing them out, and Jack offered them a little smile and nod. Once they grabbed a couple beers for themselves, they joined the table, citing how a few more of their old schoolmates were planning to show after learning Ethan was back.

Shawn was glad to see Ethan's earnest smile, when he learned who they were, so Shawn allowed himself to relax. He didn't need to protect Ethan, not here, not from these people. Smiling, Shawn leaned over and nuzzled his nose into the crook of Ethan's neck.

By the time the band was ready to play, the Horseshoe seemed near bursting. They also had more company with two more square tables pushed up against their own. Surrounded by old friends, Ethan didn't seem to mind the crowd. That, of course, eased Shawn's own worries.

"You okay?" Ethan inquired all the same when he noticed how quiet Shawn had become. Shawn forced a little smile, nodding as he snuggled against Ethan's side. That made Ethan grin, pressing a kiss to Shawn's temple.

"Y'know, it's kinda sweet when yer like this," Ethan mentioned. Shawn scowled at him in protest. "And yer cute when you get all growly too," he added, cutting off Shawn's retort with, "Lemme make *you* feel better for once."

At that, Shawn's face softened, and he relaxed against Ethan. "Alright," he murmured, nose nestled at Ethan's neck once again.

Shawn was more than content to stay like that. He didn't know most of what the band was playing, although he had to admit they sounded good. Nor did he know any of the people they were hanging out with. Therefore, simply being cozied up to Ethan, occasionally drinking his scotch and listening to what everyone was talking about, was fine by him.

Of course, that was in between all the hollering for the band, Ethan making good on his promise to keep the energy alive. They also stopped conversation at random to sing along to a particular song, and some of the group went off to dance. Even Ethan slipped away at one point, joining in on some line dancing of all things.

"This is for all those lovebirds out there tonight," Matt announced when they reached the end of their first set, smiling pointedly at Ethan before striking up the opening chords.

* * *

Ethan smiled softly, tugging at Shawn's hand and finding he went easily. Shawn grinned down at Ethan as he was pulled in close to him on the dance floor. The gentle melody drifted over them, Matt's voice crooning to yet another popular country song, "Wanted."

Unlike at the Greyson's party, Ethan was completely at ease. He took ahold of Shawn's hand, his other one pressing at Shawn's lower back to drag them together so they touched along their entire bodies. Shawn's hand came up and rested between Ethan's shoulder blades, allowing Ethan to lead him.

It was just a rhythmic rocking back and forth as they turned, but with Shawn in his arms, it was the best thing in the world. Ethan rested his nose on Shawn's cheek, not able to help the little smile on his face. Without meaning to, his voice mixed with Matt's during the chorus, feeling the answering smile as Shawn gave him a squeeze.

Ethan moved his head back to gaze into Shawn's gray eyes, not for the first time counting himself extremely lucky to have found this man. Everything except the music faded away, lost in the moment of simply holding each other. Shawn's lips quirked before he leaned in and stole a kiss.

As Shawn tried to move away, Ethan refused to let him go. He took Shawn's face in both his hands, drawing him into a more passionate kiss as the music crescendoed into the chorus once again. Ethan tugged at Shawn's lower lip with his teeth when he ended it, eyes flicking up to meet Shawn's as they fluttered open.

A grin split across Shawn's face that brightened up the whole room. Shawn cupped the back of Ethan's head, pressing their foreheads together while they continued to sway to the music, neither able to stop smiling.

When the final chords were playing, Shawn put his mouth next to Ethan's ear and whispered, "I love you."

Ethan nuzzled against his cheek as he replied fondly, "I love you too."

While everyone else clapped, cheered, and whistled for the band, they found it hard to pull away. Ethan glanced up at his brother on stage, noting Matt beaming at them. Ethan could only shake his head, offering Matt a thumbs-up. He gave Shawn one more lingering squeeze and suggested they grab fresh drinks at the bar before joining the band on their break.

"Sex on the beach?" Ethan teased with a raised brow after they ordered. "Really?"

"What? They're good," Shawn defended. He leaned in, expression turning smoky. "Unless you were hoping it was an offer."

"I think it's a little cold for that."

"Aww, come on," Shawn continued to prod, hand brushing across Ethan's hip. He was only playing around of course; Ethan knew that.

"Not big on exhibitionism, hon." They were both smiling as Ethan leaned in to press a quick kiss to the corner of Shawn's mouth.

"Great. The fag's back in town."

Ethan turned his gaze to the source of the graveled voice.

"Didn't we get rid of you?"

"See they didn't take out the garbage while I was gone," Ethan huffed back, moving to square his body better against the trio that, by the looks of them, had just walked in.

Mason and his moronic friends had been a source of many problems growing up. There were homophobes all over town, except most adults bit their tongues to Ethan's face and talked behind his back. Kids were cruel. With it being a small town, everyone knew everyone else's business, so it wasn't as if it had taken long for word to spread about his sexuality. The bullying had followed soon after.

"Cute." Mason took a good look at Shawn before sneering at Ethan. "This your little boy toy?" Mason looked between his lackeys, Kyle and Noah, as they all laughed. "Oh wait. It's probably you takin' it up the ass, am I right?" Shawn's brows lowered, hands curling into fists. "Think he'd mind if we borrowed that pretty little mouth of yours for the night?"

Ethan scoffed, shaking his head as he acted like he was turning away. Instead, he simply caught Mason off guard. His fist hit Mason's face with a satisfying *smack thud* on impact. Ethan moved to the right, popping up with his left fist to connect with Kyle's jaw, followed by a jab that threw Kyle back against the bar.

Shawn wasn't as inclined to play fair. He nailed Noah right in the balls, slapping his palms sharply over Noah's ears to disorient him. Shawn then caught Mason's fist that was clearly meant for Ethan's face. With a sharp movement, Shawn jerked Mason's arm backward, forcing him to bend over and then kicking at the back of Mason's knee.

"Next time I see you," Shawn growled, "I'll rip out your spleen and feed it to the wolves."

That even made Ethan's brows rise, and it certainly did the job with Mason. "Okay, okay, I'm sorry. *Fuck*. Please let go." Shawn gave one further yank before doing just that, shoving Mason away and watching him curl up on the floor in pain.

Shawn's eyes narrowed on Noah and Kyle, both throwing their hands up as they inched toward their downed friend. They were too scared to try anything more. Noah was holding his head while Kyle worked his jaw back and forth, both wincing at the pain their own wounds caused.

"You three get the fuck out of here!" the owner, Danny, ordered from behind the bar. "I don't tolerate that shit in my place!"

"They started it!" Kyle growled back, blood dribbling from his nose. Noah was picking Mason off the floor, looking at least somewhat remorseful.

"Fuck off and don't lemme catch ya in here again!" was all Danny replied, not having time for their excuses. "Like I ain't got eyes and ears," he added under his breath.

Ethan watched the trio like hawks as they stumbled all the way out the door. When it was clear they were gone, he turned to Shawn with a mix of elation and gratitude on his face. "Dude, you surprise me more and more each day."

Shawn waved it off, reaching for Ethan's hands to look them over and make sure they were still in one piece. "They had it coming," Shawn replied. Satisfied Ethan was okay, he met Ethan's eyes again and quirked his lips. "Damn, I haven't been in a bar brawl in years."

Ethan barked out a laugh. "Come on, old man. Let's get back to it, huh?"

They gratefully accepted their drinks 'on the house' from the bartender, shaking their heads ruefully at Matt's ramblings of awe when they joined them at their table.

Ethan smiled fondly over at Shawn. All the love Ethan had was shining in his eyes as he laid his hand over Shawn's, catching his gaze as well as the returning grin.

* * *

The last few days at Sweetwater Ranch seemed to fly by. Between going horseback riding with the Brant men and staying up late drinking hot cocoa in front of the fire with Aileen, it was an experience Shawn would never forget.

When the ball dropped on New Year's Eve, Shawn for once found himself surrounded by a caring family. It wasn't that Sophia somehow didn't count. However, to be there where everyone was actually filled with real love for each other, accepting of who they were, was a novelty.

As he accepted the warm hug from Aileen out on the porch, Shawn honestly was tempted to stay. He realized why Ethan had said he wouldn't return to Cape Cascara if he had gone home after the accident. The Brant's were stability and love, a heady thing for the likes of Shawn.

"Thanks for having me," Shawn managed to tell her, smiling down at the strong and fearless woman that he'd come to admire.

"You're welcome here anytime, Shawn." She gave his bicep a squeeze.

"Take care of my boy, now," Henry added, offering his hand.

"Promise."

"Heard that, Dad," Ethan mock-complained, passing by with the last of their bags to be packed in the car. It was a wonder that they had arrived with three bags but were leaving with a full load in tow.

"We're allowed to worry, bro," Matt threw in as he followed behind. "Not that I'm likely to after seeing Shawn kick ass at the bar."

"Yes," Ethan replied dryly, "he defended my honor perfectly." Shawn only rolled his eyes.

"Jus' sayin'... I'm impressed."

While the siblings continued to discuss the damsel-in-distress scenario, Aileen pressed something into Shawn's hand. "Case you ever need a bed, honey."

It was a house key, and Shawn knew without being told that it was to the ranch. He didn't know what to say, so instead, he nodded, holding back the emotion choking up his vocal cords. Aileen seemed to understand anyway, giving him a gentle smile as she wrapped her arm around Henry's waist.

"Be careful on the drive home," Henry instructed.

It was Ethan who replied, "Yes, sir," as he joined them. "We'll call you when we get back."

"And rest stops," Aileen added as his parents pulled Ethan into a shared hug. She pressed a kiss to his hair when he agreed.

"Love you, kiddo," Henry said as Ethan tucked himself closer to them in an attempt to drag things out. Not that Shawn was about to rush him.

"See ya 'round," Matt said to Shawn, offering his fist.

Shawn bumped it with his own, smiling a little. "Spring break," he reminded Matt.

"Alright, bro," Matt complained, knocking Ethan on the shoulder. "Where's the love for me?"

Ethan turned right around, picking his brother off the ground in a bear-hug and causing everyone to chuckle. "Don't get into too much trouble without me, Matty."

A final round of good-byes was said, and they were on their way, a bittersweet feeling in Shawn's chest at leaving the ranch behind. However, their lives and homes were waiting for them in Washington.

There was no telling if that would change someday. Tomorrow could bring anything, really.

* * *

They were on a long, lonely stretch of road. With no illumination other than the headlights, Ethan was able to see the vast array of stars stretching out across the heavens. Head against the window, he smiled up at the sky.

"Y'know, when I was a teenager, I saw a shooting star," Ethan said, conversationally.

"Yeah?" Shawn glanced over at him, lips turning up at the corners when he saw the dreamlike look on Ethan's face. "Did you make a wish?"

"Of course."

When Ethan didn't offer anything further, he prompted, "And what was it?"

Ethan looked at him then, smiling tenderly. He slid his hand into Shawn's as he answered, "I wished that I would be happy. That I would be surrounded by my family and the man I loved...and be happy." He squeezed Shawn's hand. "Looks like my wish came true."

Shawn felt his chest tighten, warmth spreading over him. "Well, I'll do my best to keep it coming true." All he could do was smile when Ethan leaned over, nestling into his side as best he could, given their current positions, head laying on Shawn's shoulder.

"Get some sleep," Shawn urged. "We'll be home soon."

Home. Ethan smiled against his shoulder and murmured, "Already there."

ABOUT THE AUTHOR

Author of gay romantic fiction, from contemporary to paranormal and everything in between.

For Casey, existence equals writing. History nerd, film enthusiast, music lover, avid gamer, and just an all-around geek. Add in an unapologetic addiction to loose-leaf tea and you get the general picture. Married, with furry four-legged children, Casey lives happily in the middle of nowhere Ohio.

Facebook: https://www.facebook.com/authorcaseywolfe
Tumblr: http://authorcaseywolfe.tumblr.com
Website: https://authorcaseywolfe.wordpress.com
Goodreads: http://www.goodreads.com/authorcaseywolfe
Email: AuthorCaseyWolfe@gmail.com

NineStar Press, LLC

www.ninestarpress.com

www.ingramcontent.com/pod-product-compliance
Lightning Source LLC
Chambersburg PA
CBHW020341260626
47156CB00004B/1629